THE

DOCTOR WHO
THE AMBASSADORS
OF DEATH

Based on the BBC television series by David
Whitaker by arrangement with the British
Broadcasting Corporation

TERRANCE DICKS

Number 121 in the
Doctor Who Library

TARGET

Published by
the Paperback Division of
W.H. ALLEN & Co. PLC.

A Target Book
Published in 1987
By the Paperback Division of
W.H. Allen & Co. PLC
44 Hill Street, London W1X 8LB

First published in Great Britain by
W.H. Allen & Co. PLC 1987

The BBC producer of *The Ambassadors of Death* was Barry Letts,
the director was Michael Ferguson
The role of the Doctor was played by Jon Pertwee

Typeset by Phoenix Photosetting, Chatham
Printed and bound in Great Britain by
Anchor Brendon Ltd, Tiptree, Essex

ISBN 0 426 20305 4

CONTENTS

1

'Something Took Off From Mars . . .'

Far above the Earth, in the infinite blackness of space, two metal capsules were converging.

It had taken immense amounts of money, vast quantities of highly complex technical equipment, untold hours of dedicated and highly-skilled work to bring these two capsules to this point, where they were almost – not quite – ready to link up.

In the cramped control cabin of the capsule that had not long ago taken off, Senior Astronaut Charles Van Leyden was listening to the instructions of Mission Control, which in this instance was just outside London.

In a deep, heavily accented voice, Mission Control was saying: '. . . and starboard course correction one degree. Are you reading?'

Van Leyden, a stolid-looking fair-haired young man replied calmly, 'Reading okay. One degree. Now.'

He touched a control, very briefly. 'Manoeuvre completed.'

In the command chair at Mission Control, Ralph Cornish glanced at a read-out screen, and frowned briefly.

Cornish was quite literally tall, dark and handsome. He was vaguely aware of his good looks, though he considered them more of a handicap than anything else. His voice was deep, calm, well-modulated, and radiated confidence and reassurance: 'You overshot, Charlie. Make a two second correction to port.'

Equally calm, Van Leyden's voice came back: 'Two second correction to port – now.'

Cornish reflected wryly that Van Leyden, like himself, wasn't nearly so relaxed as he sounded. Otherwise that second course correction would never have been necessary.

There was now just the faintest edge in Van Leyden's voice as he said, 'Error rectified.'

'You're doing fine, Charlie,' said Cornish soothingly.

'What's my distance from Mars Probe Seven?'

Cornish spoke into a desk-mike. 'Distance computation, please.'

The heavily-accented voice of Bruno Taltallian came from the speaker: 'Distance five hundred and eighty miles. Seven minutes three seconds to objective.'

Then Van Leyden's voice acknowledged the message. 'Confirm.'

Cornish spoke again, pitching his voice in the same smooth, almost hypnotic tone. 'Charlie, how's it going?'

'No problems. Everything's fine.' Again the faint edge in the voice. 'Still no radio contact?'

Cornish's calm reply confirmed what Van Leyden and everyone else knew very well. 'Charlie, there's been no radio contact with Mars Probe for seven months.'

'Then how do we know they're still alive?'

'They took off from Mars manually, Charlie,' said Cornish patiently. 'They must have been alive then.'

'*Something* took off from Mars . . .' Van Leyden said flatly.

The massive bearded figure of Bruno Taltallian came lumbering in from Computer Control. He glanced up at the giant monitor screen in front of Cornish, on which he could see Van Leyden hunched tensely over his controls. 'How's it going?'

Cornish flicked the cut-off switch. 'They're closing. Charlie's a bit edgy.'

Taltallian shrugged his burly shoulders. 'Can you blame him? It's very possible he's going up to rendezvous with a flying coffin.'

A tall trimly-moustached figure in military uniform came into the control room in time to hear this last remark. Brigadier Alastair Lethbridge-Stewart, Commanding Officer of the United Nations Intelligence Taskforce (British Section), looked very hard at the impassive Taltallian, then turned to Cornish. 'Do *you* think they're dead?' he asked.

'I don't know,' Cornish said. 'But in seven months space time, you'd think they could have fixed a defective radio.'

Taltallian spoke his thoughts with his usual brutal frankness: 'If they are dead it will turn public opinion against our European Space Programme.'

Cornish shot him a scornful glance. 'Frightened your computer grant will be cut, Bruno?'

Taltallian gave one of his typical shrugs and turned away.

'What are you going to tell the public?' asked the Brigadier curiously.

With a hint of relief in his voice, Cornish turned back to his monitor screens. 'Fortunately, that's not my job.'

The man whose job it was to inform the Great British Public was installed in the VIP viewing room just off the control room watching events through the huge glass window.

As always he was perfectly relaxed and at home, just as long as he was standing – or, in this instance, sitting – in front of a TV camera.

Michael Wakefield was a small, neat, bearded, bespectacled bow-tied man with the low, throbbing, earnest voice that seems to be the exclusive property of a certain kind of TV journalist. It was a voice that conveyed expertise, sympathy, concern and a sort of muted reproach. The implication was that somehow Michael Wakefield already knew all the answers. Luckily for him, he never had to provide them. He only asked the questions, and passed along the background information assembled for him by an expert team of researchers, all kept firmly behind the camera.

He was talking now with his usual air of reproachful concern . . . 'In a few minutes we shall know the answer to the question that has been occupying the minds of everyone here at Space Control, ever since Mars Probe Seven took off from the red planet on its return journey nearly eight months ago.' Wakefield paused dramatically. 'What has happened to astronauts Frank Michaels and Joe Lefee?' Another pause. 'Communications remained perfect on the long journey out to Mars, and throughout the difficult landing. For a full twelve hours they sent back pictures and reports from the surface of the planet. Both then seemed to be in perfect health. Then' – the most dramatic pause of all – 'silence!'

Wakefield's earnest face was filling TV screens all over the country, and one of them was in a big old-fashioned room in an old-fashioned building not too far away. It was an extraordinary-looking room in its way, a mixture of past, present, and, in a sense, future.

The solid-looking whitewashed brick walls and the huge port-hole-like circular stained-glass window suggested the architectural style of the turn of the century. Crystal chandeliers and a dresser loaded with assorted ornamental cups and plates and vases confirmed the impression.

Yet, another wall was lined with metal shelves containing an amazing jumble of scientific equipment, both electronic and chemical. Nearby stood a cluttered old-fashioned roll-top desk.

Most amazing of all was the many-sided control console that dominated the centre of the room. A transparent column rose from its centre, and each facet of the console was crowded with rows of instruments, dials, monitors and switches.

A very tall, very thin man in a ruffled shirt and an elegant black velvet jacket stood staring thoughtfully at the television screen. His trim build and his erect posture suggested a man at the peak of his fitness, yet the hair was completely white, and the handsome autocratic face was neither young nor old.

This was the Doctor, a wanderer in time and space whose wanderings had temporarily come to an end.

Exiled to Earth by his own people, the Time Lords, he was currently occupying the post of Unpaid Scientific Advisor to UNIT. To enforce his exile, the Time Lords had immobilised the TARDIS, the Doctor's space/time craft, and taken away his memory of time travel theory in order to prevent him from repairing it.

A rebel by temperament, the Doctor spent much of his time trying to escape his exile. For this reason he had taken the central control console from the TARDIS and installed it here in his UNIT laboratory, where he spent much of his time attempting to get it working again.

The television coverage of the return of Mars Probe Seven had temporarily distracted him from this activity, but a few minutes of Wakefield's dramatic mannerisms irritated him to the point where he could stand no more. Reaching out a long arm, the Doctor

11

switched off the sound, leaving Wakefield mouthing silently, and went back to the TARDIS console to resume his work.

An auburn-haired girl in a brown wool dress and sleeveless cardigan came in from an adjoining room and stood watching him for a moment. Extremely intelligent, and good-looking in a rather severe sort of way, she was called Liz Shaw. Liz was a top-ranking Cambridge scientist, shanghaied by the Brigadier into being the Doctor's assistant.

At first the collaboration hadn't worked all that well. Liz was too highly qualified to be anyone's assistant, and the Doctor was too conceited to admit that he needed one. But by now, after sharing two dangerous adventures, they were beginning to develop a wary mutual respect, and even liking.

'What are you doing, Doctor?' she asked crisply. Her tone implied that whatever it was, it was probably childish and nonsensical.

The Doctor replied curtly, 'I'm trying to repair the TARDIS's time vector generator.'

'And what's that supposed to do?' She wandered over to the console, studying it with her usual air of sceptical amusement.

There was a dangerous gleam in the Doctor's eye as he explained, 'Well, for one thing it could send you into the future if it starts working again – and particularly if you're standing there!'

Liz laughed in his face. 'Oh, come on now, Doctor . . .'

The Doctor flicked a couple of switches. The TARDIS console made a sudden wheezing, groaning sound, and Liz disappeared.

'Liz!' called the Doctor in alarm.

Looking a little startled at the accuracy of his own prediction, the Doctor frantically flicked more switches. 'Good grief!' he muttered. He operated more controls and Liz reappeared – just as the Doctor himself suddenly vanished.

Startled, Liz looked round. 'Doctor, where are you?'

She started to move around the console and vanished – just as the Doctor appeared in her place.

Puzzled by her absence, the Doctor too looked round. 'Liz?' He flicked more controls, there was another wheeze from the console and Liz reappeared. 'Ah, there you are,' said the Doctor satisfied. He went on with his work.

'What happened?' demanded Liz.

'Well, we both got caught in the time warp field and were projected into the future.'

'*Into the future?*'

'Yes, but only about fifteen seconds,' said the Doctor calmly, consulting his watch.

'But I haven't been anywhere,' protested Liz. '*You* vanished.'

'No, no, no,' said the Doctor impatiently. 'You vanished first. I only seemed to have vanished because you went into the future and I wasn't there yet. Trouble is, the wretched thing seems to have packed up again. Still, we're on the right lines.'

Liz gave him a baffled look and was about to argue further, but the Doctor was looking at the screen of his still-silent television set.

It showed the scene at Space Control, and prominent in the foreground was a familiar military figure.

'There's the Brigadier,' said the Doctor indignantly. 'What's he doing at Space Control?'

'Apparently something's happened to the Mars Probe.'

The Doctor snorted. 'Well, I suppose he's got to do something to occupy himself now that he's blown up the Silurians.'

The Doctor was referring to a race of intelligent reptilian beings, he'd discovered living below the surface of the Earth. They had considered their claim to the planet to be superior to that of mankind. The Brigadier, following his duty as he saw it, had dealt with the menace by entombing the Silurians in their caves – an act for which the Doctor found it hard to forgive him.

Liz gave the Doctor a reproachful look, but decided against re-opening the argument. Instead she turned the sound up again, and Wakefield's sonorous tones filled the room: '. . . and you can see from the radar screen – that's the screen just to the left of Professor Cornish – that the recovery capsule and Mars Probe Seven are now close to convergence. This is a tense moment for Controller Ralph Cornish and his team. The two craft will be linking up in just a moment or two, and then we shall know the answer to the question – and indeed the mystery – that has been baffling the world's scientists for the past seven months . . .'

The giant monitor screen in front of Ralph Cornish's command console was still filled with a close-up of Van Leyden in the cramped cockpit of his recovery capsule.

Cornish leaned forward in his chair. 'Charlie, do you have visual contact yet?'

Van Leyden's voice came back over the speaker. 'Not yet. I'm changing the attitude of the capsule.' He adjusted controls and the picture tilted a little.

Van Leyden glanced out of the nearby porthole. 'I can see it. I'm right up alongside.'

Cornish gave an inaudible sigh of relief, but his voice remained as calm and confident as ever.

'Well done, Charlie, everything looks good.'

The Brigadier leaned over his shoulder. 'Ask him if

it's definitely Mars Probe Seven.'

Cornish swung round. 'What?'

'Ask him.'

Turning back to the screen, Cornish said, 'Charlie, can you give us definite identification? It *is* Mars Probe Seven?'

A little puzzled, Van Leyden replied, 'No doubt about it. I can see the markings.'

'Fine,' said Cornish, a little too heartily. 'Charlie, do you hear anything from them?'

They saw Van Leyden operate controls, then listen for a moment. He shook his head. 'Still nothing.'

'Try to contact them once more, before link-up.'

'Okay.'

Cornish looked up at the others. 'Maybe the transmitter's too weak to reach us down here. Maybe Charlie . . .'

He broke off as they heard Van Leyden's voice from the speaker. 'Recovery Seven to Mars probe. Do you read me? Am about to initiate link-up. Do you read me?' Van Leyden looked out at them from the screen. 'Still nothing, Ralph. I'm going to rotate for link-up now.'

'Go ahead, Charlie.'

In the blackness of space the two cone-shaped capsules seemed to drift gently towards each other, narrow end to narrow end like two halves of some oddly shaped dumb-bell.

In the Control Room at Space Control, everyone was listening intently to Van Leyden's calm voice.

'Buffeting slightly . . . I'm firing port retro-jets to compensate. Moving in for link-up – *now*.'

(The two halves of the dumb-bell came closer, closer, and then locked neatly together . . .)

This time there was more than a hint of triumphant relief in van Leyden's voice. 'I have link-up!' he cried.

Cornish, too, was calmly jubilant. 'Well done, Charlie. Everything's looking fine.'

'Activating locking clamps now . . .'

Liz Shaw returned to the UNIT laboratory, a mug of coffee in each hand.

She found the Doctor still hunched absorbedly over the television set, as if he wanted to climb inside to the Control Room. Putting one mug down, she tapped him on the shoulder. 'Thought you weren't interested?' she said, and handed him the other mug of coffee.

The Doctor gave her a reproving look. 'They've just linked up.'

'Any signal from Mars Probe Seven?'

'Not a sound . . .'

'All right, Charlie,' said Cornish gently. 'Talk us through.'

'Injecting air into tunnel – now.' Van Leyden's voice came over the loudspeaker. In the dead silence of the Control Room they could hear the faint hiss of air as Van Leyden pressed a control and the tunnel was pressurised.

'Is the air holding, Charlie?'

'Air pressure in tunnel okay. Am moving to locking clamps . . .'

They saw Van Leyden unfasten himself from his chair and float gently across the tiny cabin to a circular door. On the other side was the connecting arm of the dumb-bell – the tunnel that joined the two linked capsules.

'Releasing first clamp . . . first clamp away. Second clamp . . . Suddenly Van Leyden's voice rose with excitement. 'I can hear something!'

Cornish's voice was calmer than ever. 'What is it, Charlie? What do you hear?'

'I think they're opening their hatch. It's them! Third clamp away. I am now removing hatch preparatory to entering tunnel . . .'

Everyone in Space Control had their eyes riveted to the giant screen.

They saw Van Leyden spin the locking wheel, and the door swing open.

They saw Van Leyden disappear into the tunnel, like some cumbersome space-suited rabbit down its hole . . .

(In the gloom of the tunnel, Van Leyden saw a shape drifting towards him. He stared hard as the shape came closer, and suddenly Van Leyden's welcoming smile changed to a grimace of unbelieving horror.)

An unearthly sound rang through the Control Room at Space Control, relayed from the two linked capsules drifting in space.

A high-pitched electronic screech, it seemed to echo round the brains of everyone who heard it, paralysing all thought . . .

In curiously similar gestures, Cornish, Taltallian, the Brigadier, all clutched their hands to their heads in a vain attempt to block out the intolerable howl.

Mercifully it stopped, and they stared at each other, shaken and confused.

Cornish was the first to recover. 'Charlie what's happening?' he cried down the mike. There was no reply. 'Control to Recovery Seven, do you read me?'

There was nothing but silence, and the unending *beep* . . . *beep* . . . *beep* of the communication system . . .

The Doctor sat staring at the TV set like a man hypnotised.

'Doctor, what is it?' asked Liz alarmed.

The Doctor gave her an anguished stare. 'That sound . . . I've heard it before . . .'

2

'That Sound – It Was Some Kind Of Message . . .'

Liz stared at the Doctor in utter amazement. 'Heard it before? How? When?'

The Doctor slapped a hand down on his knee with a crack like a pistol-shot. 'That's just it. I don't know. I can't remember!'

'What do you mean, can't remember?'

The Doctor sprang to his feet. 'Don't you understand? The information's in my mind but I can't reach it.'

Although Liz didn't realise it, the explanation was simple enough. In taking away the Doctor's knowledge of time travel theory, the Time Lords had perforce interfered very considerably with his memory. These days, the Doctor frequently had the infuriating experience of not being able to make use of his own memories.

By now the Doctor was already heading for the door. 'Come on, Liz, I think we'd better go there right away.'

'Go where?'

'The Space Centre, of course, it isn't far away . . .'

The Doctor rushed out, and Liz hurried after him.

Minutes later they were rocketing towards Space Control in Bessie, the Doctor's souped-up Edwardian roadster. They arrived just as the barrier at the gate was being raised for some official limousine.

Before the barrier could be lowered again, the little yellow car nipped through like a sprat in the wake of a whale, and disappeared inside the complex.

Meanwhile, not much had been happening inside Space Control. The screen had gone blank and the speaker was silent. Only the radar screen was still functioning, showing the two capsules, linked together, hanging in space.

Cornish sat in his command chair repeating the same phrase over and over again in an inhumanly calm voice. 'Hello, Recovery Seven, do you read me?'

He must have said it a hundred times by now, and was clearly prepared to say it a hundred more.

The Brigadier interrupted him. 'Can't you send up another recovery capsule?' he asked.

Cornish glanced briefly at him. 'Not immediately.' He returned to his console. 'This is Control to Recovery Seven. Do you read me?'

In a corner of the control room, Wakefield was conducting an interview with an irascible Bruno Taltallian, who would say only that communication had broken down, it often broke down in cases such as this, and no, he had no idea of what the strange sound might have been.

Forced, not for the first time, to make news out of the fact that there was no news, Wakefield wrapped the interview up. 'So, until the situation becomes clearer, the world must wait and hope . . .'

The Brigadier had very little more luck with the brisk white-coated Miss Rutherford, Cornish's assistant, who told him that an excessive power build-up in the solar batteries *might* have caused the problem, and that Van Leyden *might* be able to unlink and bring Recovery Seven back down despite the communication breakdown.

Baffled and powerless, the Brigadier almost welcomed the distraction of raised voices outside the control room. One of them was very familiar . . .

'My dear fellow, I simply don't happen to have a

pass. As a matter of fact, I don't approve of them!'

The Doctor swept into the room, trailing a protesting security guard and a pacifying Liz Shaw in his wake.

He paused at the top of the little flight of steps that led down into the main body of the control room, and glared accusingly at the Brigadier. 'Ah, *there* you are!' A security guard reached out to grab the Time Lord from behind. 'Take your hands off me!' The Doctor snapped.

'It's all right,' said the Brigadier hurriedly. 'I can vouch for these people.'

The baffled security man withdrew, and the Doctor swept magnificently into the control room, Liz at his heels.

The Brigadier returned the Doctor's glare. 'What are *you* doing here?'

The Doctor marched up to him. 'That sound – have you heard it again?'

'No.'

'You will.' The Doctor strode determinedly towards Cornish in his command chair.

'He says it's a message, Brigadier,' explained Liz.

'Who from?'

Liz shrugged helplessly, and the Brigadier turned to the Doctor, who was looming over Cornish.

'Have you got a recording of that message?' demanded the Doctor.

Cornish didn't even look up. 'I'm sorry, I've no time to talk to the Press.'

'Quite right,' said the Doctor approvingly. 'Neither have I. Now, that sound – did you take a recording of it?'

'Everything here is recorded,' said Cornish wearily. 'Brigadier, please – '

The Brigadier tried to bustle his Scientific Adviser away. 'Now, Doctor, everybody's got a great deal to do here – '

'No, they haven't. There's nothing anybody can do for the moment.'

'Brigadier, who *is* this?' demanded Cornish angrily.

'One of my associates.'

'Then kindly get "one of your associates" out of here!'

'Come along, Doctor,' said the Brigadier hopefully.

The Doctor ignored him. 'That sound was some kind of message, and it's going to be repeated.'

'Could you *please* get this man out of here?' repeated Cornish. We're trying to save the lives of those three astronauts.'

'Nonsense, man,' said the Doctor. 'You're doing nothing of the sort. You can't possibly do anything until – ' He broke off as an agonising electronic howl filled the control room.

Just as before, everyone clapped their hands over their ears in a vain attempt to block out the sound. Everyone, that was, except the Doctor, who stood listening, head cocked, with an expression of keen interest.

'High frequency accelerated sound,' he said thoughtfully, when the howling at last died away. 'He turned to Cornish. 'Right, I shall need multi-copies of the recording, unlimited computer time and somewhere to work. Miss Shaw, you'd better stay and help me.'

The Doctor looked hopefully at Cornish, as if expecting his requests to be met without delay.

Cornish stared thoughtfully back at him. 'How did you know that sound would be repeated?' he asked curiously.

'By exercising my intelligence. Since we didn't reply, they would obviously repeat the message. We've got to break the code and answer them.'

'Answer who?'

The Doctor turned to the Brigadier. 'The man's a fool! How can I tell who the message is from until I know what it says?' He spoke to Cornish in the way one would address a very small child. 'Let me explain in simple terms . . .'

Cornish seemed about to explode, and the Brigadier intervened hurriedly: 'He *is* trying to help, you know, Professor Cornish. You *might* find him quite useful.'

The Doctor threw himself up. '*He* might find *me* useful?'

'I mean, Doctor, that you could help Professor Cornish.' The Brigadier glared meaningfully at the Doctor and added pointedly 'He *is* in charge here, you know!'

'Hmm,' said the Doctor. He swung round on Cornish and beamed at him. 'My dear fellow, do forgive this intrusion. You really must let me decode that message, you know. It could be of vital importance to the safety of your astronauts.'

Suddenly, Cornish felt the full impact of the Doctor's personality, a blend of formidable intelligence and tremendous charm. He heard himself saying, 'Well, I suppose we ought to try everything. Though how you can be so sure . . .'

The sound came again, or rather, another version of the sound, less intense and therefore more endurable, but more long drawn out as well.

Cornish looked up at the Doctor. 'It seems you were right. I'll see about that computer time . . .'

He reached for the telephone but the Doctor said, 'No, not just at the moment.'

'I thought you wanted to crack the code and send a reply?'

'That was the reply,' said the Doctor simply. 'Brigadier, can you arrange for world-wide triangulation right away?'

23

The Brigadier was puzzled. 'But we know where the transmissions were coming from, Doctor. From the capsule in orbit.'

The Doctor shook his head. 'The first ones, yes, but not this last one. *That* was completely different, and we've got to find out where it was coming from.'

'I'll get on to it right away.'

As the Brigadier moved away to a wall-phone Cornish said, 'But aren't we too late now, Doctor?'

'The message was repeated, so perhaps the reply will be too. All we can do now is wait.'

Michael Wakefield was concluding yet another of his 'no news is bad news' broadcasts. 'And so, after seven and a half months of total silence: these mysterious transmissions for which scientists here have no explanation – though one theory is that they may be some kind of distress signal. It is now some hours since the last communication from the capsule, and unless the link-up can be restored it is difficult to see what can be done – short, of course, of sending up another recovery craft . . .'

In the control room the Doctor and Liz, assisted by the Brigadier, were checking off a number of triangulation points on an illuminated screen upon which was projected a large scale map of the world.

'Haystack, Algonquin, Arecibo, Cambridge . . .' said the Doctor, and as he spoke, the Brigadier studied the map and duly checked off points in Massachusetts USA, Canada, Puerto Rico and England.

Meanwhile the hulking form of Bruno Taltallian was looming over Professor Cornish. 'I have computerised the factors involved in sending up another recovery capsule,' he announced.

'What's the minimum time for blast-off?'

'Ten days.'

'That's unacceptable,' Cornish said flatly. 'They'll have to speed it up.'

As the argument raged, the Brigadier ticked off Vorograd and said thankfully. 'That seems to be the lot.'

'Tokyo have just promised full co-operation,' said Liz.

The Doctor nodded approvingly and studied the map. 'Well, if the transmission's from Earth this should give us the country. But that's not accurate enough. We must pin-point the exact location . . .'

He looked up as they heard raised voices from across the Control Room. 'Recovery Eight was not scheduled for launch for another three months,' Taltallian was bellowing.

'They'll have to speed it up,' snapped Cornish.

'But you know they have problems with the new fuel injection system . . .' Bruno Taltallian broke off, covering his ears, as that intolerable electronic screech filled the Control Room yet again.

This time it was mercifully brief, but brief as it had been, the transmission had been picked up and recorded by a network of radio tracking stations across the world, and within minutes the Doctor and his friends were busy at the map as the reports came flooding in . . .

Liz handed the Brigadier yet another bearing. 'From the observatory at Nancy . . .'

The Brigadier drew another line with his chinograph pencil on the glass screen that covered the map. It went through the focal point where other similar lines intersected.

The Doctor looked at the map and rubbed his chin. 'London,' he said softly. 'It's coming from London!'

He began flicking controls on the map screen and was

25

rewarded with a detailed picture of the surface of the Moon. He marched across to Cornish and waved indignantly at the screen. 'Can I get a map of London on that thing? It's rather urgent.'

Cornish, who was still wrangling with Bruno, said wearily. 'That machine will give you a surface map of every surveyed planet, but a map of London – no!'

The Doctor shook his head despairingly. 'Useless gadget!'

'Doctor, never mind the map,' called the Brigadier. 'My people have just done a local triangulation.'

The Doctor swung round eagerly. 'What's the exact location?'

The Brigadier sounded as if he couldn't quite believe what he was saying. 'An abandoned warehouse, Doctor – on the outskirts of London . . .'

3

'They'll Never Survive . . .'

On the upper floor of that warehouse, in the room that had once been the manager's office, two men sat before a complex piece of radio apparatus.

One, clearly the senior in both age and rank, was a sparely-built middle-aged man with short hair, a neatly trimmed moustache and the kind of expensive Savile Row suit that is almost a uniform in itself. He wore a red carnation in his buttonhole. His name was Carrington.

The second man – the one actually operating the set – was a powerful-looking thick-set young man with close cropped fair hair and a heavy moustache. His name was Grey.

'Run the message again,' ordered Carrington. 'Give it all the power you've got.'

Grey looked dubious. '*Full* power, sir?'

Both men knew what was involved. The stronger the signal, the greater the risk of detection.

'Full power,' said Carrington firmly. 'We'll have to risk it . . .'

Three UNIT Land-rovers crammed with armed soldiers sped through the seedy streets of one of the poorer parts of West London.

The Brigadier sat in the passenger seat of the leading vehicle consulting a folded map. 'That's it – there!' he said, pointing. 'Through that archway.'

The driver swung the steering wheel of the Land-rover and they shot through a sort of narrow tunnel set between two massive abandoned buildings. The rest of the little convoy followed.

The archway led into a huge cobbled yard and there at the far end was the old warehouse, a massive, old-fashioned building with row upon row of arched windows, every one methodically broken by the industrious local vandals.

To shouted orders from officers and NCOs the UNIT troops leapt out of their vehicles. Their boots clattered on the cobbles, as the men fanned out, covering the entrances of the building. Revolver in hand, the Brigadier led the main party through the big front door, which was gaping open.

The electronic howl of the alien signal filled the little upstairs office.

Grey glanced worriedly at Carrington who said finally, 'That's enough.'

The signal died away as Grey switched off. 'Do you think anyone was monitoring us, sir?' he asked anxiously.

'Sure to have been. But finding us is another matter.' As Carrington spoke the door burst open and a huge, roughly-dressed man with bristly crew-cut hair and a thick moustache rushed into the office. 'Sir – UNIT's outside!'

'How very efficient of them,' said Carrington almost admiringly. He rose. 'Keep them off as long as you can, will you, Collinson?'

'Yessir!' snapped Collinson. Drawing a heavy service automatic, he ran from the room.

'Try not to kill anyone – unless it's absolutely necessary,' called Carrington after him. He turned to Grey. 'Send the final transmission.'

'Have we time sir?'

'The sergeant will hold them off.'

'Yes, sir.' Grey switched on the apparatus.

The alien sound once again filled the air . . .

The Brigadier led his men into a massive, cavernous building, high-ceilinged and longer that it was wide.

Iron pillars supported the roof, and here and there the vast open space was dotted with old packing cases and chunks of rusting machinery. At the far end of the warehouse was an internal staircase that went up to the floor above. The Brigadier led his men towards it.

Or rather he started to – when suddenly a bullet ricocheted off an iron pillar close to his head. He caught sight of a figure ducking into cover at the other end of the hall.

'Enemy ahead – take cover – fire at will!' he shouted, and dived for the protection of that nearby pillar.

In the brief confused fire-fight that followed the Brigadier and his men should have had it all their own way. There were more of them, for a start, and they were armed with automatic rifles. The enemy, which appeared to consist of no more than a handful of civilians, seemed only to have automatics.

But they were using them with astonishing skill. The Brigadier watched in amazement as one of his men was sent staggering back by a bullet that struck the butt of his rifle, while another was left clutching his fingers as a bullet in the trigger-guard sent his weapon flying from his hands.

As the battle went on the Brigadier became aware of two things. One: the enemy were simply better than his own men, better shots, better trained in this kind of house-to-house fighting. Who on Earth were they, he wondered. Some elite, foreign-trained terrorist squad?

Two: the enemy, whoever they were, weren't really trying. True, they protected themselves from the fire of the Brigadier and his men, flitting from one piece of cover to another, dissolving into the shadowy gloom like so many ghosts. But for all the deadly accuracy of their firing, nobody was being hit.

The Brigadier leapt from cover, and blazed away at the enemy, shot after shot. The unseen enemy fired in reply. Bullets whined and buzzed around him but not a single one hit him.

There was something rather humiliating about fighting an enemy who weren't even trying to hit back. With a yell or rage, the Brigadier led his men in a charge towards the enemy.

The two groups clashed not far from the flight of steps. To his astonished rage, the Brigadier discovered that even in hand to hand combat his men were outmatched.

All around him UNIT troops were being deftly kicked, punched, tripped, and sent flying through the air by enemies who vanished into the shadows.

The Brigadier was about to hurl himself into the struggle when he became aware of a massive figure running swiftly to the internal staircase. He leapt forwards, levelling his freshly-loaded automatic. 'You can stop right there!'

The big figure paused, then turned slowly around – until the automatic in his hand was covering the Brigadier.

'Better put it down,' said the Brigadier quietly.

'You're probably right.' But the automatic in the big man's hand was unwavering.

The Brigadier glanced round, and saw that most of his men were already picking themselves up. 'You kill me, my men kill you. Pointless really.'

'Since you put it like that . . .' But still the automatic was covering the Brigadier.

Just behind the big man, a dazed UNIT soldier was

getting to his feet. He took in the situation, and saw too that a heavy porcelain insulator-coil was dangling from the ceiling nearby.

Stealthily he got to his feet, drew back the insulator and aimed it so that it would smash into the back of the big man's head.

Seeing what was happening, the Brigadier yelled, '*Now!*'

'The soldier released the coil, which swung through the air, but the big man, alerted by the Brigadier's shout, swung round and ducked so that the swinging weight missed him. The UNIT soldier tried to grab him and the big man chopped him to the ground. He dashed forwards, barging past the Brigadier and sending him flying, and jolting him so hard that the weapon clattered from his hand.

The big man darted for the stairs and the Brigadier ran after him. Once again the man swung round, aiming his automatic at the Brigadier.

The difference was that this time the Brigadier was unarmed. The big man smiled wryly at his adversary for a moment as if savouring his triumph. Then he opened his hand and let the automatic fall.

It clattered to the ground. Thankfully the Brigadier snatched it up.

He gestured to a couple of his men to take the captive away, and called the others to follow him. It was about time he found out what was at the top of that staircase – and who was sending signals to the astronauts.

In the little office, Carrington was gathering up papers. He slid a bolt across the door. 'Trigger the self-destructor unit.'

Grey moved to the specially modified set and pressed a button. Something clicked, and the set began ticking.

'Out you go,' ordered Carrington. Grey opened the window and clambered out onto the fire escape.

As the sound of booted feet came up the stairs, Carrington drew an automatic and fired a few shots deliberately wide of the door.

The footsteps stopped. A voice called, 'All right, open up!'

Carrington smiled and climbed through the window after Grey.

The Brigadier kicked open the door and burst in, his automatic in his hand. He looked round the empty room, saw the open window and the fire escape beyond and sighed.

He turned and saw the ultra-modern radio, incongruous in the dusty deserted office.

He was just thinking that they ought to learn something from the radio when it blew up . . .

The Doctor had been absent from Space Control for a while, much to Cornish's relief. Now he was back, storming across the room and up to Cornish's command chair, a tape-spool in his hand.

'Now, see here, Professor Cornish, I can't possibly help you people unless you give me full co-operation.'

'What's the trouble, Doctor?' asked Cornish wearily.

'I've already told you – computer time. If I'm to decode those messages I need a computer.'

'Then go and see Doctor Taltallian – computers are his department.'

'Yes, so he's just informed me, but he's being totally non-cooperative.'

Cornish sighed. 'I'll talk to him.'

He touched a control, and a mini-screen rose up from his console. The bearded and bristling face of Bruno

32

Taltallian appeared on the screen.

Before he could speak Cornish snapped, 'Bruno, I told you to give the Doctor *full* co-operation. See that he gets it.'

Cornish touched the control again and the still-spluttering Taltallian disappeared. Cornish looked up at the Doctor. 'Satisfied? Now, if you'll excuse me?'

Cornish showed irritation so seldom that it was all the more effective. A little non-plussed the Doctor said, 'Er, yes,' to no one in particular, and joined the waiting Liz at the door.

Cornish, meanwhile, was staring at a recently-arrived message. 'Athens have sighted a solar flare building up – a big one.'

Miss Rutherford gasped. 'When? When do they expect it?'

'Any time in the next twenty-four hours.'

'The astronauts will never survive the solar flare radiation,' she said worriedly. 'You'll have to bring them down on remote control.'

'I can't. They're still locked on manual,' said Cornish dully. 'There's nothing I can do.' He leaned forward and began repeating the familiar litany. 'Control to Recovery Seven, do you read me? Athens have just reported a dangerous solar flare build-up. It is imperative that you unlock manual control so we can bring you down. Recovery Seven, do you read me?'

Cornish's voice crackled through the control cabin of Recovery Seven: 'I repeat, we have a message from Athens Observatory. A massive solar flare is building up. The flare is expected at any time during the next twenty-four hours. Are you reading me Recovery Seven? Are you reading me?'

But there was no one to reply to Cornish's message, or even to hear it.

The cabin of Recovery Seven was empty.

Armed with Cornish's backing, the Doctor and Liz marched determinedly to the main computer control room, the heart of Taltallian's empire.

'Right,' said the Doctor happily. 'We'll see what he's got to say for himself this time!'

He flung open the door, and marched into what appeared to be an empty room.

The door slammed behind them and they saw the room was not empty after all. Bruno Taltallian had been standing behind the door.

Before they could ask him the reason for his odd behaviour, he did something even odder.

Snatching a gun from underneath his white lab coat, he pointed it straight at the Doctor . . .

4

'Recovery Seven – It's On The Way Back!'

The revolver was trembling in Taltallian's hand. 'I want that tape, Doctor!'

The Doctor looked at the tape-spool in his hand as if he'd forgotten he was carrying it. 'Ah yes, the tape. Do you realise the importance of it?'

'Rather more than you do, Doctor.'

'So, you understand the message?'

Taltallian ignored the question. 'Hand it over.'

'What are you going to do with it?'

'Doctor, give me that tape!'

'Since you insist.' The Doctor stretched out his hand, Taltallian lunged forwards, and the tape disappeared.

'This is no time for conjuring tricks, Doctor,' snarled Taltallian. 'Raise your hands.'

The Doctor raised his hands and Taltallian patted his pockets one by one. But he found nothing. '*Where is that tape?*' he demanded.

'Perhaps he sent it into the future?' suggested Liz, remembering her earlier experience with the TARDIS console.

'Doctor, are you trying to force me to shoot you?' Taltallian asked furiously.

The door opened and the Brigadier entered. 'Doctor, I – ' He broke off. For a moment he stood astonished at the spectacle before him, then reached instinctively for his own automatic.

Immediately the gun in Taltallian's hand swung to cover him.

'Careful, Brigadier,' warned the Doctor. 'He's frightened.'

The Brigadier nodded, taking his hand away from his holster. Nothing was more dangerous than a gun in the hand of a frightened man who was unused to firearms.

Taltallian turned the gun on Liz. 'You, come here.' With his free hand, he grabbed Liz's wrist and twisted her arm brutally behind her, then edged towards the door, using Liz as his shield. 'Don't try to follow me!' he cried.

Shoving Liz away from him, he darted through the still open door, and slammed it shut behind him. With a yell of 'Guards!' the Brigadier dashed in pursuit.

The Doctor went over to Liz who had fallen to her knees in the centre of the room. He helped her to her feet. 'Are you all right?'

'More frightened than hurt. What about Taltallian?'

'I think we can safely leave him to the Brigadier.'

'What did you do with the tape? You didn't send it into the future, did you?'

'Tape?' said the Doctor absently. 'Oh, the tape. Here it is!' He stretched out his hand and suddenly the tape was back again. 'No, no, no, that was simply transmigration of object,' he explained, referring to a Time Lord technique somewhere between telekinesis and conjuring. 'There's a difference between that and pure science, you know. Now, what about cracking this code?' The Doctor surveyed the humming computer technology around him with a slightly bemused air.

Tactfully Liz took the tape from his hand. 'Here, let me. That'll be the digital analogue converter over here.' She slotted the tape into the maze of machinery.

The Brigadier panted back into the room. 'He got away – this place is a rabbit-warren! I've set up a search.'

The Doctor nodded, and dismissed Taltallian from his thoughts. 'What did you find at that warehouse?' he asked the Brigadier.

'A transmitter.'

'And?'

'We took a prisoner. He knows a great deal more than he's saying.'

'I'd like to have a talk with him. Can you cope here, Liz?'

Liz's scornful look was reply enough. The Doctor grinned, and followed the Brigadier from the room.

Now kitted out in a set of army fatigues, the Brigadier's prisoner lay stretched out on his bunk in a UNIT cell. He got to his feet as the door opened and the Doctor and the Brigadier entered the cell.

The Brigadier glared indignantly at him. 'Well, have you decided to talk yet?'

Clearly the prisoner had not, since he said nothing at all.

'Why didn't you shoot me when you had the chance?'

Still no reply.

'Why don't you sit down, old chap?' the Doctor suggested gently. Suspiciously, the prisoner sat on the edge of his bunk, and the Doctor continued. 'You were under orders not to harm the Brigadier and his men, weren't you?' The Doctor had been given a full account of the events at the warehouse on the way over. 'Who gave you those orders?'

'I can't answer questions,' the man replied gruffly.

The Doctor turned to the Brigadier. 'Find anything on him?'

'No, his pockets were empty. His clothes were the sort of thing you can buy anywhere, with all the labels cut out.'

'Very thorough,' said the Doctor drily.

Despite more questions from the Doctor – and more threats from the Brigadier – the man refused to say any more.

'It's no use,' said the Doctor at last. 'We're wasting our time, Brigadier.'

'But this man must know something.'

'Yes, but he's not going to tell us anything. We've got more important things to do.'

The Brigadier rapped on the door, a guard corporal opened it and the Brigadier left the cell. The Doctor followed, then turned and came back in again.

He beamed at the prisoner. 'Looking after you all right, are they? Had a cup of tea?'

The prisoner looked baffled. 'Yes thanks.'

'That's good . . . STAND TO ATTENTION WHEN YOU TALK TO ME AND CALL ME SIR!' bellowed the Doctor, with the parade-ground rasp he'd learned at Waterloo.

With an answering bellow of '*Sah!*' the prisoner sprang to his feet and to attention in one smooth, well-drilled movement.

The Doctor grinned 'I thought as much. Sergeant, aren't you?' Caught out, the prisoner relaxed, and slumped down on to his bunk.

The Brigadier came back into the cell. 'A soldier? A deserter?'

The Doctor shook his head. 'No, no. I think he's still acting under orders . . .'

A UNIT soldier entered the cell and handed the Brigadier a note. He studied it, then looked up astonished. 'Recovery Seven – it's on the way back!'

For once Wakefield had some real news to communicate, and he was making the most of it.

'There has been another extraordinary development in the mystery of Mars Probe Seven; he said into his microphone. The two capsules which, for some time, have been locked together in radio silence have now

38

separated, and Recovery Seven appears to be returning to Earth. However, there is still no communication between Earth and Charles Van Leyden, or from astronauts Michaels and Lefee.'

The Brigadier and the Doctor marched into Space Control.

'Still no word from them?' asked the Doctor.

'Nothing,' said Cornish, turning back to his console-mike. 'Recovery Seven, do you read me?'

A voice from the tracking area came over a loud-speaker. 'Tracking report. Capsules now approximately seven miles apart.'

'We're eleven minutes from scheduled re-entry blast-off,' said Miss Rutherford quietly.

Cornish gave her a rueful look. 'I wish I had your confidence.'

'Tracking report,' said the speaker again. 'Distance between capules increasing. Nine miles, thirteen miles . . . twenty-five miles.'

'It's the re-entry blast-off,' said Miss Rutherford urgently. 'They've started!'

'Ten minutes too soon,' muttered Cornish. 'What does he think he's doing?'

There was a flurry of activity in Space Control as the assembled technicians checked instruments and discussed the new event in low voices.

The Doctor turned to the Brigadier. 'Well, that's it for a while. I'd better see how Liz is getting on with the decoding.'

'Don't you want to see what happens to Recovery Seven?'

'If they're going to attempt re-entry they'll make at least one Earth orbit. I'll be back in time. Coming, Brigadier?'

'No, I think I'll start a security trace on our prisoner.'

As the Doctor and the Brigadier left in different directions, the loudspeaker voice came again. 'Recovery Seven speed now eighteen thousand miles per hour and increasing. Capsule will leave our radar range within three minutes, closing to two point nine five.'

'Notify global tracking stations,' ordered Cornish. 'Fix an open communications circuit. I want that capsule tracked every second.'

Even as the Brigadier was on the telephone setting up his security trace, steps were being taken to remove his prisoner from captivity.

The guard bringing the prisoner his meal froze as he felt the muzzle of an automatic jabbed into his back.

He swung round and a brown-gloved hand knocked the tray into his face and clubbed him expertly behind the ear. The guard fell, and the same brown-gloved hand took his eyes and opened the door of the cell.

The prisoner rose, grinned, and headed for the open door. He had never been in any doubt about his eventual rescue. It was only a matter of time . . .

The Doctor, Liz, and a senior computer technician called Dobson were all three staring gloomily at an enormous computer print-out sheet.

'It's nonsense,' said the Doctor indignantly. 'No sign of a pattern at all.'

Dobson, a thin-faced dark-haired little man with a mournful face, shrugged his shoulders. 'Maybe we're feeding it nonsense. Maybe that stuff from the capsule was just freak static.'

The Doctor gave him a disgusted look, and Liz said

hurriedly, 'Maybe there's a computer malfunction?'

Dobson said, 'Impossible. There's a self-checking mechanism.'

'Even that could go wrong,' Liz pointed out. 'I'll feed it a test program.'

'Never mind that,' said the Doctor suddenly. 'Ask it what two and two make!'

Liz punched the sum into a computer terminal and looked at the read-out screen.

'This is ridiculous,' said Dobson as Liz waited for the answer. 'That machine was checked this morning.'

'How long have you known Taltallian?'

'Two years; I'm his chief assistant.'

'Look,' said Liz pointing to the screen. 'It says the answer's five!'

'I never did trust those things,' said the Doctor.

'This isn't a malfunction,' said Liz. 'Taltallian must have sabotaged it.'

Dobson drew a deep breath. 'Right. I'll soon have it working again . . .' He bent over the keyboard, muttering technicalities to himself.

'I'll leave you to it,' said the Doctor, and hurried off. Somebody, it occurred to him, was prepared to go to any lengths to prevent his decoding that message, and for the time being, at least, that somebody had succeeded.

Perhaps he could find some answers in Space Control . . .

5

'The Capsule Has Landed.'

The Doctor re-entered Space Control at a moment of extreme tension.

After its rough and unorthodox re-entry, Controller Cornish was desperately trying to bring the capsule safely to land. But to do this, he had to re-establish some measure of control . . .

'Capsule now in tracking and control range,' said an anxious loudspeaker voice.

'Transmitters on – now!' ordered Miss Rutherford. She leaned forward, studying her console. 'It's not responding!'

'Repeat transmission,' said Cornish calmly. 'Boost power.'

The loudspeaker voice came again. 'Tracking report. Height, ninety miles and reducing. Speed, twenty thousand and holding . . .'

'It's no good,' said Cornish, and for the first time there was defeat in his voice. 'It's still not responding.'

Even the Brigadier knew what that meant. He turned to the Doctor and whispered, 'They'll burn up!'

Suddenly a high-pitched warbling came from the transmitter.

'It's responding!' said Miss Rutherford excitedly.

Cornish was like a man given new life. All the old, quiet confidence returned to his voice. 'Recommence transmission and maintain. Fire retro-jets in five seconds.'

Miss Rutherford pointed to the radar screen. 'We've got radar contact now.'

A spot of white light was moving slowly across the

screen. It was strange to think that it represented the tiny metal capsule, hurtling through the sky, and still in danger of imminent destruction.

It was precisely this point that Wakefield was relaying to his millions of viewers; by now most of the sets in the country were tuned in to the broadcasts from Space Control.

'After what was a pretty rough re-entry by present day standards, astronauts Van Leyden, Michaels and Lefee are now experiencing the buffeting of Earth's atmosphere as their huge parachutes lower them on the last stages of their descent, in what is known as a hard landing, as opposed to the more usual splash-down. Space Controller Cornish has done a magnificent job in bringing the capsule down at all, but the question now is, exactly where will it land . . .'

This question was pre-occupying everyone in Space Control as they studied an enormous map projected onto a wall screen.

The map showed an area of Southern England, dangerously close to London itself. Cornish had aimed to bring the capsule down on a largish area of fairly deserted scrubland. With his late and limited control of the capsule's progress it had been his best, indeed his only option.

'Ground-level preparations complete?' he asked.

The Brigadier nodded. 'The whole area will be cordoned off as soon as the capsule lands. Civil airlines have been warned, and all planes diverted.'

The loudspeaker voice came again. 'Drop-speed twenty-two miles per hour, reducing. Eighteen . . . Height, one mile, drift rate, three knots . . .' A pause then, 'Contact lost, contact lost . . .'

The Brigadier looked alarmed. 'Something wrong, Doctor?'

The Doctor said reassuringly, 'They always lose contact in the last few seconds . . .'

There was another pause then the voice said, 'The capsule has landed.'

'We've made it!' cried Miss Rutherford.

'Well done, old chap,' said the Doctor.

'Congratulations, Controller,' said the Brigadier heartily. 'Wonderful job!'

Cornish buried his face in his hands for a moment. Then he looked up. '*If* they're alive . . .'

The Doctor, the Brigadier and Professor Cornish arrived at the capsule landing site as quickly as a police-escorted UNIT convoy could get them there.

They arrived just after Space Control's Capsule Recovery Team which had been waiting on full alert, and had set off for the area even before the actual touch-down.

By the time the team from Space Control had come onto the scene, the huge trailing parachutes had been gathered up and stowed away, and the capsule was already on a low-loader transporter lorry, ready to be taken back to Space Control.

A communications unit had been linked to the capsule, and Cornish was still trying to establish contact with those within.

Ironically, although he was now trying to reach them across a few feet of space and steel, rather than thousands of miles of space, he had no more success. 'Hello, Recovery Seven, do you read me? This is Cornish. You have landed safely. Open your hatch.' There was no response.

He had several more attempts before giving up. 'It's hopeless,' he despaired. 'Perhaps they're unconscious.'

'We'd better open it ourselves then,' said the Brigadier practically.

Cornish nodded and stepped back. Technicians began swarming all over the capsule, but their efforts too were in vain. 'It's no good,' said Cornish at last. 'Either the mechanism's jammed or . . .'

'Or they've locked it from the inside,' finished the Doctor.

The Brigadier said, 'We'll have to cut it open.'

'Dangerous for the astronauts.'

'Then what do we do?'

'I suggest we get the capsule back to the Space Centre,' said the Doctor. 'We can tackle the problem there.'

All this time, the capsule and the activity around it had been under close observation through high-powered binoculars. The watchers were Carrington and his aide Grey, the two men who had been operating the radio in the deserted warehouse. This time they were dressed in country tweeds as if out for a day's shooting, and indeed they were keeping watch from a shooters' hide, hurriedly constructed in a wooded hillside overlooking the capsule.

'RT,' snapped Carrington. 'UNIT frequency.'

Grey opened a shooting bag at his feet and put on the headphones attached to the RT set inside. He began adjusting the controls.

The Brigadier stood by his jeep, barking orders into the UNIT radio transmitter. 'I want a route cleared from here to the Space Centre for a low-loader with outriders. I'll give you the map reference, and our intended route . . .'

As the Brigadier spoke, Grey was listening in and taking notes. When the Brigadier had finished transmitting, Grey handed the pad to Carrington, who studied it carefully. 'Excellent. Couldn't be better . . .' Like the Brigadier, he began reeling off a string of orders.

With the capsule securely lashed to the low-loader and hidden from curious eyes by an enormous wrapping of silvery plastic, the Brigadier gave a nod of satisfaction and got in the passenger seat of the lorry, ready to lead the convoy away.

The Doctor, meanwhile, was climbing into Bessie. Much to the Brigadier's disgust, the Doctor had insisted on his ancient-looking roadster forming part of the convoy; the Brigadier couldn't help feeling it lowered the military tone.

Cornish looked through the window of the low-loader. 'I'm going directly to the Space Centre. By the time you arrive I'll have everything ready.'

As Cornish got into his car and drove away, the Brigadier leaned out of the lorry window and peered at the Doctor in Bessie. The little car was emitting an alarming variety of bangs and rattles and seemed in danger of blowing up. 'See you back at the Space Centre,' shouted the Brigadier. '*If* you make it!'

He shouted an order to the two UNIT motorcyclists ahead. They pulled out and the lorry lumbered slowly after them. The Brigadier turned to the lorry driver. 'Be sure to keep to the agreed route,' he reminded him. They've cleared the way ahead of us . . .'

With a final bang and splutter Bessie roared away, turning into a side road to get ahead of the slow-moving convoy . . .

In the cabin of the low-loader, the Brigadier settled himself for a long slow journey, reviewing the arrangements in his mind, reassuring himself that nothing could possibly go wrong. Ahead of them, unseen police cars were clearing their route to the Space Centre. The UNIT motorcyclists rode ahead to deal with any local obstruction. There were two more outriders behind, and behind them the rest of the UNIT vehicles. Nothing could go wrong . . .

The Brigadier heard a faint rumbling from overhead. Looking up out of the window, he was surprised to see a helicopter hovering just above and ahead of the convoy.

He frowned. He hadn't ordered air support. Perhaps someone at UNIT HQ had been over-keen. Still, it couldn't do any harm . . .

The helicopter zoomed lower . . . Dangerously low, so low that it seemed to be buzzing them . . .

Craning his neck out of the open window the Brigadier glared indignantly up at the hovering shape . . .

It was a biggish helicopter and there seemed to be several men on board. An arm appeared out of the helicopter door, and a round black metal object arced down towards the UNIT convoy. It hit the ground just ahead of the lorry, exploded with a dull *crump*, and emitted clouds of billowing smoke.

They were being bombed, the Brigadier realised. Smoke-bombed! Another bomb fell behind the lorry, choking the two following out-riders.

More and more smoke-bombs rained down, ahead, behind and on either side, and the whole convoy was soon engulfed in choking black smoke.

The low-loader jolted to a halt and the Brigadier leapt out, drawing his revolver. Through the swirling smoke he could see the dim shapes of the motorcyclists ahead, bringing their machines to a halt.

And he saw something else, a huge round shape dropping to the ground, just on the edge of the smoke haze.

The helicopter was landing.

It seemed to hover inches above the ground and two grotesque shapes leapt out. They wore drab coveralls and plastic face-masks and they had twin cylinders lashed to their backs. From the cylinders a length of tubing was connected to oddly-shaped nozzled guns in the attackers' hands.

As the helicopter hovered, waiting, the two men ran towards the convoy.

The leading motorcyclists tried to bar their way, and as the Brigadier watched in horror, the weirdly-dressed attackers raised their strange weapons and blasted them down.

'Gas-guns!' thought the Brigadier, as the two motorcyclists staggered back choking and fell to the ground enveloped in white smoke.

The attackers were already running towards him. The Brigadier had time for only one wildly-aimed shot before a choking cloud of gas swallowed him up and he collapsed unconscious.

The rest of the battle was soon over. The two remaining outriders zoomed up from the rear and were shot from their machines. One by one they parted company from their bikes, flew through the air and collapsed unconscious.

The UNIT troops from the following vehicles ran forwards firing, and they too were shot down by the gas-weapons. One of the two attackers ran to the lorry, knocked out the driver with a quick gas-blast, hauled him from the driver's seat and took his place.

The second attacker was already climbing into the passenger seat from the other side, and seconds later the lorry was jolting slowly away.

Satisfied that the operation had been successfully concluded, the helicopter pilot put his machine into its almost vertical ascent.

A last remaining UNIT soldier, who had somehow managed to escape the gas guns, fired at the helicopter, missed, dashed towards it and actually managed to cling onto the landing gear as the helicopter started rising.

He clawed his way up to the still-open door and was half-way inside when the pilot's boot shoved him savagely away, and he fell to the ground, rolling down a steep bank but miraculously surviving unhurt.

Free of his weight, the helicopter zoomed upwards like a lift. Far below, the pilot could see a litter of crashed motorbikes, stalled vehicles and unconscious men, while the lorry carrying the capsule rolled slowly down the road . . .

After making the necessary adjustments to Bessie's souped-up but sometimes erratic engine, the Doctor sped on his way through the quiet country lanes.

The country was relatively flat and the hedges low, and the Doctor was considerably surprised to see the shrouded shape of the capsule moving along above a distant hedgerow, particularly since it was moving in quite the wrong direction.

Thoughtfully the Doctor spun the wheel round, made a neat racing turn and raced off to intercept the wandering lorry.

In the cab of the lorry, Carrington and Grey had shed their masks and gas-guns and were doing their best to look like a couple of drivers on a routine delivery.

They were astonished to see, as they swung around the next bend, that an ancient-looking Edwardian roadster was slewed across the road, barring their way.

Grey leant out of the driving window and called, 'Will you get out of the way, please? We're carrying a very important cargo.'

The owner of the vehicle, an eccentric-looking white-haired individual in a flowing cloak, was peering inside the old car's open bonnet. Straightening up, he spoke in a quavery voice. 'If you want me out of the way you'll have to give me a hand. Old Bessie seems to have stalled.'

Carrington and Grey exchanged glances. The old car was a light enough model to be shoved manually out of the way, and after that the old fool could look after himself.

They jumped out of the cab and ran towards the roadster. Getting behind the old car they began shoving it to one side.

The Doctor watched them with benign interest for a moment. Once the car was pushed clear of the road, he reached under the dash-board and flicked a switch marked *Anti-Thief Device*.

There was a high-pitched alarm sound, and suddenly the two men found themselves glued to the car, unable to pull their hands away. They heaved furiously, but somehow they were held, fixed like metal attracted to a powerful magnet.

'Thank you, gentlemen,' said the Doctor, in a voice that wasn't quavery at all. Don't worry, you may be able to break free – eventually!'

Watched by the helpless, furious men, the Doctor climbed into the cab of the lorry, started the engine and drove off in the direction of the Space Centre.

6

'They've Started To Crack The Code . . .'

The Brigadier and Controller Cornish were walking along the corridor that led to the hangar which had been prepared to receive the capsule.

The Brigadier was trying to explain what had happened. He had woken up, like his men, some considerable time after the attack, angry and humiliated, but otherwise unharmed.

Now he was trying to tell Cornish about the catastrophes. But astonishingly enough Cornish appeared not only unbelieving, but positively uninterested. 'A helicopter, Brigadier? Smoke-bombs?'

'Yes, they were very well organised,' said the Brigadier wearily. 'What you don't seem to understand, Controller, is that we've lost the capsule and the Doctor as well. So you see – '

They came through into the main hangar and the Brigadier broke off in amazement. There in the centre of the hangar was the capsule, and standing beaming in front of it was the Doctor.

'How on Earth . . .' spluttered the Brigadier.

'*I* brought it here, Brigadier!'

'Thank goodness you're all right. We found you're car – I thought they must have got you.'

'Didn't you find two angry men stuck to my car?'

'No, just the car,' the Brigadier said, puzzled.

The Doctor frowned. 'I can't have got that force-field strong enough yet.'

The phone buzzed and the Doctor picked it up automatically. 'Liz? Yes, all right, I'll come right over.' He put down the phone. 'I'll tell you all about it later,

Brigadier. Liz thinks she's on to something.'

Helplessly, the Brigadier watched the Doctor sweep out. 'Do you think you can make contact, Controller?' he asked Cornish.

'I'm not sure. New equipment is being connected now.'

Accepting that somehow the Doctor had pulled off yet another miracle, the Brigadier settled down to wait.

The Doctor was studying a computer print-out, watched by Liz and the computer technician Dobson.

'You're quite right, Liz,' announced the Doctor. 'This is a definite attempt at some form of pictographic communication.'

Dobson studied the swirl of symbols. 'They could be just random patterns,' he said, unconvinced.

'With this symbol repeated *here* and *here* and again *here*?' The Doctor shook his head. 'And with *that* symbol recurring *four* times?'

Liz studied the print-out. 'Who on Earth would send a message in this form?'

'No one, Liz. No one on this Earth – but an alien intelligence so different that perhaps this is the only way it could communicate with us.'

Liz stared at him. 'Doctor, you don't really think – '

'I think it's time the Brigadier and I had a talk with someone at the top,' announced the Doctor. He strode from the room, and after a helpless glance at Dobson, Liz followed.

As soon as they had gone, Dobson crossed to a wall-phone and obtained an outside line. He dialled a number, waited, then, said, 'This is Dobson. They've started to crack the code . . .'

*　　　*　　　*

After a top-speed journey to Whitehall, the Doctor and the Brigadier had more or less forced their way into the offices of Sir James Quinlan, the newly-created Minister for Science and Technology.

Now they were trying to make Quinlan, an immaculately-suited, neatly-moustached, conventionally-minded politician, realise just how serious the situation really was. The Brigadier had just finished recounting the extraordinary behaviour of Doctor Taltallian. 'Checked and double-checked, like everyone else on this project. Yet he sabotages his own computer, draws a gun on the Doctor and runs away like a criminal.'

Quinlan shook his head unbelievingly. 'Extraordinary! I've known Bruno Taltallian for years.'

'That's beside the point,' said the Doctor dismissively. 'The question is, how many others in high places are involved?'

'I can see the reasons for your concern,' said Quinlan soothingly. 'But you have got the capsule back now, haven't you?'

'It's back,' said the Doctor savagely. 'Back and safely installed at Space Control. But the astronauts refuse to come out.'

Quinlan rose. 'I shall initiate a top-level enquiry immediately Brigadier. Now, I'm sure you'll excuse me? You must be wanting to get back to the Space Centre.'

'Is that all you're going to do?' demanded the Doctor. 'Sweep it under the carpet?'

'Come along, Doctor,' said the Brigadier hurriedly. 'I'll keep you informed, Minister.'

'I should be most grateful, Brigadier. Thank you, gentlemen.'

Quinlan watched as the Brigadier led the fuming Doctor from the room. Once the door had closed behind them, he waited a minute or two longer, then went to the door of his inner office and opened it.' 'You'd better come in,' he called. 'Won't you sit down?'

Muffled conspiratorially in hat, coat and scarf, the burly, bearded form of Bruno Taltallian came into the room and sank wearily into a chair. 'So, they have got the capsule? What went wrong?'

'I don't know yet. They've started to crack the code as well.'

Taltallian shifted uneasily. 'They're getting too close. You will have to hide me.'

'You can stay here in the Ministry, Doctor Taltallian. What could be safer?'

Taltallian nodded grudgingly. 'And what will you do about all this?'

Quinlan smiled. 'It's already been done – while they were talking to me here. They've got quite a surprise coming . . .'

Liz was helping the Controller at the newly installed communications equipment when the Doctor returned to the capsule hangar.

'Recovery Seven, do you read me?'

'Any response yet?' asked the Doctor.

Cornish shook his head. 'Nothing. I don't think there's much hope now.'

'Then I suggest we cut it open,' said the Brigadier.

Cornish nodded, accepting the inevitable. 'I've got men with thermal lances standing by.'

Suddenly there was a crackle from the speaker. 'I think I'm getting something,' said Liz excitedly. 'Hello, Recovery Seven, do you read me?'

'Hello, Space Control. This is Recovery Seven . . .'

Overjoyed, Cornish almost snatched the mike from

Liz's hand. 'Hello Recovery Seven, this is Ralph Cornish. Charlie, you're back at Space Control. Open the capsule . . .'

'We are not cleared for re-entry.'

'Charlie, you're back at Space Control . . . What's wrong in there? Open the capsule!'

After a pause, Van Leyden's distorted voice came again. 'Hello, Space Control. This is Recovery Seven. Will you clear us for re-entry please?'

The Doctor took the mike from Cornish. 'Let me try . . . Hello, Van Leyden, what is the capital of Australia?'

'We are not cleared for re-entry.'

'How many beans make five?'

'We are not cleared for re-entry.'

The Doctor put down the mike and turned to Cornish. 'Cut it open!'

They all waited tensely as the thermal lance team in their protective suits and masks cut away the capsule door and lifted it clear.

Cornish ran to the capsule, climbed the entry ladder and peered inside. He turned round, his face a picture of shocked astonishment. 'It's empty!' he gasped.

The Doctor stared at him. '*What*? Let me see!'

He climbed the ladder on the other side and peered inside. The tiny control cabin was empty.

'But we were talking to Van Leyden,' said Cornish dazedly.

'Liz, try them again,' called the Doctor.

Liz went to the console. 'Hello, Recovery Seven, do you read me?'

Once again they heard Van Leyden's voice. 'Space control, this is Recovery Seven. Will you clear us for re-entry, please?'

The Doctor pointed to a black box at the base of the empty command chair in the capsule. 'A tape recorder.'

'Triggered off by our voices,' said Cornish.

'Then where are the astronauts?' demanded the Brigadier.

'Somebody wanted us to believe they were still inside,' said the Doctor thoughtfully. 'I take it that recorder isn't standard equipment, Professor Cornish?'

'No, of course not.'

'Then somebody put it there to delay our opening of the capsule.'

'Why should anyone want to do that?' asked Liz.

'To gain time. The astronauts were in that capsule when it landed and they've since been removed!'

'That's impossible,' said the Brigadier. 'That capsule's been guarded all the time.' He looked at Liz and the Controller. 'You two know that; you've been here all the time as well.'

'Except for when your chaps turned everyone out for that security check, Brigadier,' said Cornish.

'*What*?'

Liz nodded. 'That's right. They sent everyone right away while they checked the area.'

The Doctor looked at the Brigadier. 'I take it you didn't order this search?'

'I most certainly did not!'

'There you are then. These people just turn up, clear the area, then take away the astronauts at their leisure.'

Cornish still looked dazed. 'But who'd want to kidnap three astronauts?'

'Perhaps the people who replied to that coded message?' suggested the Doctor.

The Brigadier nodded grimly. 'I think I'll go and have a word with my guard commander.'

As the Brigadier hurried away Liz called the Doctor to her side.

'What is it?' he asked.

56

Liz pointed. 'Just look at that geiger counter. The whole interior of the capsule is highly radioactive. If anyone was in there – they're as good as dead . . .'

7

'You Must Feed Them Radiation –
Or They'll Die!'

The laboratory was brand-new, constructed rapidly but efficiently in an army Nissen hut on the edge of a top secret Government Research Institute.

It consisted of a radiation room with a large immensely thick glass window at one end of the hut, and a control room filled with monitoring instruments that occupied the rest of the available space.

Inside the radiation room were three large slabs, unpleasantly like those in a mortuary. On each side lay a space-suited figure. The darkened glass visors of their helmets concealed their faces. The chests of the three figures rose and fell with their laboured breathing.

A thin white-coated scientist called Heldorf was studying a monitoring console. He had a pleasant face and thinning curly hair. He had been a refugee many years ago and his voice still held traces of a foreign accent. He looked through the window of the radiation chamber. 'Two million rads . . . They should be dead by now.'

The man beside him said quietly, 'But they're not.'

'We tried to remove their helmets but they resisted violently.'

'I told you not to remove their protective clothing!' snapped the second man. He was medium-sized, wore a clipped moustache, and was dressed in the uniform of a British Army General.

Heldorf said, 'You don't understand. These men need a complete blood transfusion, antibiotics, cortisone injections. We must reduce the radiation.'

'No,' snapped the General. 'You must increase it.'

'Are you mad?' Heldorf was shocked. 'That would be murder.'

'The radiation affecting these men is something totally new to us. In surviving it, they have become dependent upon it.'

'That is contrary to everything that I understand about radioactivity, General.'

'You must feed them radiation – or they'll die!'

'You can't ask me to do that!'

The man in general's uniform said, 'Professor Heldorf – I am not *asking* you . . .'

The Doctor and the Brigadier, this time accompanied by Liz, were having a second interview with Sir James Quinlan.

'I don't think you'll be able to sweep this under your Ministry carpet,' the Doctor was saying. 'Someone in authority must be responsible.'

Quinlan turned to the Brigadier. 'The astronauts were in your charge.'

'They were taken from the Space Centre by a squad of soldiers, under the command of two officers.'

Quinland shrugged. 'Imposters, obviously.'

'No. Their papers of authorisation were checked and found genuine. They had a platoon and an army vehicle of the latest design – not the kind you pick up in an army surplus store.'

Quinlan sighed. 'You've been very thorough, Brigadier. What a pity you have no explanation to offer for these strange occurrences!'

'We haven't come here to offer explanations,' said the Doctor crisply. 'We've come to demand them – from you!'

Quinlan stared into space for a moment then said unexpectedly, 'Very well.'

The Doctor stared at him. 'You mean you're actually going to tell us the truth?'

Quinlan smiled. 'No. But I'm going to introduce you to the man who can.' He rose and opened the inner door. 'Come in, please.'

A dapper figure in army uniform came into the room, sparsely built, trimly-moustached, Army from head to toe.

Instantly the Brigadier was on his feet and at attention. The newcomer was in the uniform of a full General.

Smugly Quinlan said, 'Allow me to present General Carrington, head of the newly formed Space Security Service.'

'Space Security?' said Liz. 'Weren't you an astronaut – on Mars Probe Six.

Carrington gave her a quick modest smile. 'Yes, I was, actually. Do sit down, Brigadier.'

The Brigadier sat, and Carrington sat down too, looking round the little group. 'I realise I owe you all an apology. I can only ask you to believe that everything I have done has been in the interests of us all.'

The Doctor wasn't to be so easily talked round. 'Does that include sending coded messages to Mars Probe Seven?'

'Not to mention Doctor Taltallian holding a gun on us in the computer room,' added Liz.

Carrington gave her another of his diffident smiles. 'Doctor Taltallian was under strict orders to ensure that you didn't have access to the computer.' He looked round the room. 'You see, every astronaut is issued with a secret emergency code, only to be used in the most ultimate emergency – the code you have been trying to break. The message we received from Mars Probe Seven told us that the capsule had passed through a hitherto unsuspected, high-density radiation belt.'

'Why didn't you inform Space Control at once?' asked Liz.

'Security.'

'Then why wasn't I informed – sir?' demanded the Brigadier.

'Because UNIT is an international organisation and the Government wishes to keep this matter in its own hands.'

The Doctor sighed. 'But why all this extraordinary behaviour? Surely radiation is a normal hazard of space travel?'

Carrington paused impressively. 'We believe this radiation to be different. We believe it to be self-sustaining and highly contagious. It could spread like a plague, contaminating the entire planet.'

'We don't want the public to become panic-stricken,' added Quinlan ponderously.

'Don't the public have a right to know?' asked the Doctor mildly. 'I believe you call it democracy.'

Carrington smiled. 'Democracy can have disadvantages, Doctor. What we are doing is for the best.'

'I see,' said the Doctor sardonically. 'It seems to be a case of the left hand fighting the right, doesn't it, Brigadier?'

Carrington chuckled, as if assuming that the incident was closed. He rose. 'Well, I hope this explanation has eased your minds, gentleman, *and* Miss Shaw.'

The Brigadier and Liz and Quinlan all rose too, but the Doctor remained obstinately seated. 'It hasn't eased mine.'

Carrington swung round, his voice dangerously calm. 'I'm sorry?'

'I should like to see these mysteriously radiated astronauts if I may.'

'I don't think that will be necessary,' said Carrington. 'They're in expert hands.'

The Doctor remained obstinate. 'Nevertheless, I should like to see them.'

Carrington frowned. For all his polite almost deferential manner, it was clear that he didn't care for opposition. Quinlan said quickly, 'I don't see that it would do any harm, General.'

Suddenly Carrington was all smiles again. 'Of course not. I'll take you there now, Doctor. I can assure you the astronauts are perfectly safe.'

In the Government laboratory the door to the radiation room was open wide and the three space-suited figures were filing out.

Heldorf and his assistant looked on helplessly – helplessly because three armed men were standing over them. Two of them were burly thugs, mercenaries with faces like stocking-masked identikit pictures. The third, the tall man in the white overall and cap was a different and more dangerous proposition altogether.

His name was Reegan, and he had been born in Ireland, though he had spent much of his life in America and other parts of the world, frequently on the run from the law. He had begun his criminal career robbing banks for the IRA, and had left Ireland in danger of his life when it had been discovered that he was keeping more of the proceeds for himself than he was donating to the Cause.

After that, Reegan had gone into business for himself, with a great deal of success, dealing in kidnapping, extortion and murder for hire. By now he was a hardened mercenary criminal, completely merciless and without any kind of scruple.

Heldorf looked on in horror as what he regarded as three sick men in his care were taken from him. 'Who are you people?' he demanded. 'Where are you taking them? If you take them away from here they'll die. You mustn't do this . . .'

'Shut up,' said Reegan, with cold and deadly finality. He turned to the two henchmen. 'I'll see you outside – when you've finished here.'

Reegan followed the three space-suited figures outside. Suddenly Heldorf realised the meaning of Reegan's words. With a cry of protest he flung himself forwards. The nearest thug knocked him back with a brutal blow and then callously shot him down.

Heldorf's assistant grabbed a stool and raised it above his head, but the second thug shot him down, and he collapsed, the stool falling from his hands.

A large white van was parked outside the laboratory. Reegan opened the rear door and the three space-suited figures climbed into the van, as if following some pre-arranged plan.

The two thugs came out of the laboratory and Reegan said, 'You ride in the back with them.' The men looked doubtful and Reegan said scornfully, 'Don't worry, they won't hurt you. Besides, you've got guns, haven't you?'

The men climbed into the van with the space-suited figures and Reegan closed the door and locked it. He went round to the front of the van, got behind the wheel and drove away.

Minutes later, Bessie came zooming along the path between the Nissen huts. The Doctor was at the wheel with Carrington beside him, and the Brigadier and Liz in the back seat.

Carrington showed them into the laboratory, and seemed to freeze in horror at the scene before him – two dead men on the ground and the door to the radiation chamber gaping wide.

As the Doctor knelt down to examine the bodies, the Brigadier said crisply, 'Where's the phone, sir?'

Carrington pointed. 'Over there . . . Who could have done this?'

Satisfied that the two men were beyond help, the Doctor straightened up, looking meaningly at the empty radiation chamber.

'Perfectly safe, were they?'

Liz had been studying Heldorf's notes. 'Look at this, Doctor. This seems to be the radiation records of the missing astronauts – two million rads. They couldn't possibly have survived . . .'

The big white van – the legend on the side read *HEY-HOE LTD, LAUNDERERS* – was parked in an enormous gravel pit. On the other side of a huge mountain of gravel, somewhere in the distance, a crane was at work.

Reegan, now wearing a lightweight protective suit, jumped out of the front, went round the back and opened the rear doors. An arm flopped out and Reegan, apparently unsurprised, grabbed it and pulled the dead body of one of his henchmen out of the van.

Reaching inside he grabbed the dead body of the second man and hauled that out too. He heaved both bodies to the edge of the gravel pit and tumbled them over.

He went back to the van, took out the dead men's two revolvers and tossed them beside the bodies.

Then, scrambling down beside the bodies, he took papers from inside his radiation suit and stuffed them into the dead men's inside pockets.

He scrambled back up the gravel slope to a position just above the two slumped figures. Laying back against the slope he began kicking down gravel with his feet. Very soon he had started a landslide and before very long both figures were completely buried.

Reegan jumped back into the van and touched a hidden control. The van's number plates swivelled round, changing to a completely different registration, and the panel on the side swivelled too, so that it now read *SILCOX BAKERIES*.

Reegan drove off, whistling cheerfully to himself. It had been a useful exercise. Now he knew how deadly the space-suited figures really were. Besides, if they had survived the two thugs would have wanted paying, and Reegan always liked to cut down operating expenses when he could . . .

In the late Heldorf's laboratory all was bustle and activity. General Carrington was on the phone to Whitehall, the Doctor and Liz were studying Heldorf's notes, and a UNIT forensic team was scouring the laboratory for evidence under the Brigadier's supervision.

The bodies of Heldorf and his assistant had been taken away, and were now represented by the traditional chalked outlines on the floor.

Carrington came off the phone and came over to the Doctor. 'Are you getting anything useful from those notes?' he asked.

The Doctor spoke without looking up. 'Possibly.'

'Possibly?' snapped Carrington. 'Doctor, do you realise the importance – '

'I realise very well,' interrupted the Doctor. 'That is why I need to continue with my work without interference.'

'I'm so sorry,' said Carrington with that sudden diffidence of his. He moved away to hover over the UNIT soldiers as they worked.

The Doctor finished his study of the readings. 'It's quite extraordinary, Liz. According to these notes those astronauts were actually emitting radiation, like walking reactors.'

'But radiation destroys human tissue,' she protested.

The Doctor nodded. 'Yes, I know . . .'

The Brigadier's investigations had established a radioactive trail that led outside the buildings then disappeared, suggesting that the astronauts had been taken away in some vehicle.

Carrington seemed to be of the opinion that foreign agents were responsible. 'This contagious radiation could be a terrible weapon in the hands of some foreign power . . .'

'Well, Doctor, any luck with those notes?' asked the Brigadier.

'In a way,' he replied. 'I think I can tell you where your missing astronauts are.'

'Where?' asked Carrington eagerly.

'Still in orbit.'

'Nonsense! They were brought down in the recovery capsule. I saw them – in this laboratory.'

'You saw three space suits,' corrected the Doctor. 'I don't know who or what came down in Recovery Seven – but they certainly weren't human . . .'

8

'We've Got To Get That Rocket Up!'

The three space-suited figures' new home was very
similar to their previous one: the same radiation chamber with its three slabs and thick glass window, and
much the same monitoring equipment in the laboratory
beyond.

Only the building was different. Windowless with
brick walls, it was clearly an abandoned army bunker.
A flight of steps in the corner, led upwards to the
outside world.

In charge of this laboratory was a balding, ratty-faced
little man called Lennox, who had been stripped of his
post and degrees for falsifying both his experimental
results and the accounts of his college.

He was staring in fascinated horror at the three space-
suited figures on their slabs. 'They must be dying,' he
said.

Reegan was on the phone. 'I don't think so,' he said
as he waited for his connection.

'I can't deal with them here,' protested Lennox.
'They should be in an intensive care unit.'

'You have your instructions, Lennox.'

'*Doctor* Lennox, if you please.'

Reegan grinned. 'I thought they took all that away
from you?' He spoke into the phone. 'Hello, yes this is
Reegan. Everything's OK, Lennox is looking after
them. I dropped off the others on the way . . '

Reegan smiled grimly at his own black joke.

The Doctor was now trying to convince Cornish that his

incredible theory was correct. 'Whoever was kidnapped from that laboratory, it wasn't your three astronauts!'

'You really think they're still in orbit in the Mars Probe?' asked Cornish.

The Doctor nodded, and Cornish went on: 'Their life-support systems will be running down. We've got to send up another recovery capsule.'

'I'd do it as quickly as possible if I were you.'

'I'll get onto the Minister straight away,' Cornish said determinedly.

In his ornate Whitehall office, Quinlan held the phone a little way from his ear to lessen the impact of Cornish's angry tones. Then he said, 'I'm sorry, Professor Cornish, but I can't see the Goverment authorising the expenditure of so much money on so little evidence.'

'We are not talking about money, we're talking about human lives,' said Cornish furiously. 'I'm going to start full launch preparations now. Unless I get your full backing I shall call a press conference and give them the entire story.'

'I would advise you not to do that,' snapped Quinlan.

'Then you'd better make sure I don't have to, Minister.' There was a click and the line went dead.

Thoughtfully, Quinlan put down the phone. He turned to Carrington, who had been listening on another extension. 'What are we going to do?'

'We mustn't let them send up another capsule.'

'I know. But how are we going to stop them?'

'I could put Cornish under arrest,' offered Carrington.

Quinlan shuddered. 'It's gone too far for that – the scandal could bring down the Government.'

'Then it's up to you,' said Carrington bluntly.

'I can only delay them. We've got to find those missing, er . . .

'Ambassadors?' suggested Carrington.

Quinlan groaned. 'Who could have taken them?'

'Any one of our enemies,' suggested Carrington. 'Or our allies . . .'

Lennox peered worriedly through the window of the radiation chamber at the three space-suited figures.

They lay on their slabs, twitching feebly, like beetles on their backs. Even as Lennox watched, one of them rolled off onto the floor. Lennox went to the radiation chamber door and tried to open it but it was locked.

'And just what do you think you're doing?' enquired a voice behind him.

Lennox spun round to find Reegan smiling menacingly down at him.

'You've got to let me examine those men,' said Lennox hoarsely.

Reegan shook his head. 'Against orders.'

Lennox pointed to one of the monitor dials. 'Look, the radiation count has dropped drastically. They *should* be recovering.'

That's good, then.'

'But they're not. One of them's just collapsed.'

'I was hired to get them here, that's all.'

Greatly daring, Lennox said. 'Do you think you'll still get your money if they die?'

It was the one argument powerful enough to affect Reegan. He went out to his van and struggled into the radiation suit he had used earlier. Returning, he took out a key and unlocked the radiation chamber door.

'I'm not sure it's safe to go in,' said Lennox worriedly.

'You said the radiation count had dropped. I won't hang about in there.'

Lennox watched through the panel window as Reegan went over to the collapsed astronaut and tried to heave him back onto the slab.

Sitting the man up, Reegan tried to remove the black-visored helmet. The space-suited figure reacted violently, struggling to its feet and sending Reegan flying across the chamber with one flailing blow.

Then, to Lennox's horror, the astronaut swung round and lumbered towards the still open door.

Lennox turned and scuttled across the laboratory, the astronaut following remorselessly behind him. He ran up the steps and tugged at the outer door. It was locked.

Lennox turned, looking up at the space-suited figure towering over him. 'You don't understand,' he babbled. 'Can't you see, I want to help you . . .'

He flattened himself against the door, as the astronaut raised a threatening hand – and then keeled over backwards, almost falling on top of the recovered Reegan who was just at the bottom of the stairs.

As Reegan jumped back, Lennox shouted, 'You shouldn't have locked this door! I might have been killed!'

'Shut up,' said Reegan savagely. He was still shaken by his experience. He was an exceptionally big and powerful man, but the astronaut had flung him across the room like a doll. Grabbing the astronaut's shoulders Reegan lugged him across the laboratory and back into the radiation chamber and wrestled him back onto the slab. The figure seemed quite inert by now and Reegan wondered if he was dead. Maybe they'd cut his fee . . .

As Reegan came out of the chamber and began struggling out of his protective clothing, the phone rang. He grabbed it. 'Reegan. Yes . . .' He listened for quite a long time, then said, 'Isotopes? You'd better get them over here.' He slammed down the phone and turned to Lennox. 'I've just found out what's wrong with our friends here. They don't need less radiation – they need *more*!'

Cornish and the Brigadier were in the capsule hangar.

'Everything's taking just that little bit longer than it ought to,' Cornish was saying bitterly. 'I think it's got something to do with Quinlan.'

The Brigadier frowned. 'Can you prove it?'

'No.'

The Doctor entered in time to hear what they were saying. 'We've *got* to get that rocket up!'

The phone rang and the Brigadier picked it up. 'Lethbridge-Stewart. Yes . . . I see. I'll come down right away.' He put down the phone. 'Two bodies have just been found in Hertfordshire, Doctor. They died from radiation . . .'

Enveloped in the heaviest protective suit he could find, Lennox carried the metal cylinder into the radiation chamber, raised the isotope's radioactive core and beat a hurried retreat.

He closed the door behind him, and Reegan locked it.

'I feel as if I'd just murdered them,' said Lennox miserably.

'You just keep obeying orders,' advised Reegan. The phone rang and he snatched it up. 'Yes, who is it? All right, I'll open the door!'

Lennox called him back to the window. 'Look, it's working!' Inside the chamber the three figures were stirring. One sat up and looked around.

Reegan slapped Lennox on the back. 'I told you they'd be all right. They thrive on the stuff!'

There was a banging on the door. Reegan opened it to reveal a goggled despatch rider standing before him. He handed Reegan an envelope. Reegan took it without a word and closed and locked the door again.

He opened the envelop and studied the two files inside. He took a photograph from each file, glanced at them and passed them to Lennox. 'You're a sort of scientist. Know these two?'

Lennox looked at the photographs of the Doctor and Liz Shaw. 'I think I met the girl once. She was doing research at Cambridge. Why?'

'Seems they're getting in the way,' said Reegan casually. 'I've got to deal with them.'

Lennox shuddered.

The Doctor too was wearing a protective suit, studying the interior of the capsule, and taking readings with a geiger counter.

He heard movement behind him, climbed down the ladder and took off his helmet. Liz had just come into the hangar. 'It's quite extraordinary, Liz,' he said. 'The radioactive contamination has almost vanished. It was intense, but very short-lived. If we can't get Recovery Eight ready in time, we can use this capsule.'

Cornish looked up from his desk. 'Provided we can get the three thousand tons of rocket we need to go underneath it . . .'

'I've had a message from the Brigadier,' said Liz. 'He wants us down in Hertfordshire to examine those two radioactive bodies.'

'How very morbid!'

'Are you coming, Doctor?'

'Certainly not! I'm going to stay here and help to get

this capsule operational.'

'All right, I'll go. May I borrow your car?'

The Doctor fished out his keys. 'All right, but be careful. Bessie's very sensitive.'

Liz grinned. 'Don't worry, she'll be quite safe with me!'

Liz had been driving for quite some while before she realised she was being followed.

At first she couldn't quite believe it, and she deliberately changed her route, twisting and turning to shake the other car off. It clung obstinately to her tail.

Liz frowned. If cunning was no use, she'd have to see what sheer speed could do. They'd reached a long straight stretch of road now on the outskirts of London.

Liz put her foot down . . .

The Doctor felt a tap on his foot and emerged from the capsule, again taking off his helmet.

This time it was the Brigadier. The Doctor looked puzzled. 'You're soon back!'

'Not particularly. I started an hour ago.'

'But Liz went to meet you! There was a message asking us to join you . . . You didn't send it?'

The two men looked at each other, realising the truth. The message had been a fake – a trap.

'I'll get after her,' said the Brigadier, and hurried away.

Speed didn't work either, and after a long and dangerously fast chase Liz found herself forced into a dead end, a little cul-de-sac close to a fast-moving river. She screeched to a halt.

Unfortunately the area was pretty deserted. A sports field led down to the river, with a narrow bridge across it over the turbulent waters of a weir. There were people about on the far side of the bridge and Liz reckoned if she could get across it she could find help.

Jumping out of Bessie, Liz dashed across the sports field. From the corner of her eye she saw two men leap out of the pursuing car and come pounding after her.

Liz's high white boots weren't really meant for running and she made slow going over the muddy ground. Things were very little better once she reached the bridge by the weir. The concrete path was narrow and slippery and the low guard rail seemed to offer little protection from the rushing water below.

Liz was forced to slow down even further, and the first of her pursuers caught up with her. He grabbed her arm and Liz gave him a vigorous shove that sent him clean over the rail. He clutched desperately at the lowest railing, just managing to save himself.

Then the second pursuer caught up with her. Liz grappled furiously with him, but he was much stronger than she was.

With a desperate effort she wrenched herself away. But she broke free with such force that she cannoned into the low guard rail and cartwheeled over it, heading for the rushing waters below . . .

9

'Someone's Threatening To Kill Miss Shaw!'

Ironically Liz was saved by her would-be captor.

He reached down and grabbed her wrist, arresting her fall, and dragged her by main force back over the railing.

By this time the second thug had clawed his way back onto the bridge. Sandwiching the shaken Liz between them, one gripping each arm, they bustled her back towards their waiting car, where a third man, tall and elegant in an expensive trench-coat, was waiting . . .

Reegan shoved Liz down the steps of the underground laboratory. 'I've brought you some company, Lennox,' he said.

Liz stared at the frightened little man. 'Doctor Lennox!'

'There,' said Reegan consolingly. 'Someone remembers you.'

'I thought they told you to get both of them,' said Lennox with feeble defiance.

Reegan shrugged. 'The feller didn't keep the appointment. Still, this one's a scientist too, she can give you a hand.'

Somewhat to his disappointment, Reegan's orders were that his captive was to be held but not harmed. He looked through the window. 'How are our zombie friends?'

'Surviving.'

'I didn't expect them to be dancing a jig.' He turned to Liz. 'You, start making yourself useful.'

'And if I don't?'

Reegan gestured to the radiation chamber. 'I might lock you in there – with them . . .'

The Doctor and the Brigadier had been assigned a shared office at the Space Centre, where the Brigadier had set up a temporary HQ. The Doctor was going through Heldorf's notes at one of the two desks, trying to ignore Carrington, who was hovering over him.

The Brigadier strode in, saluted Carrington and sat down. 'I've issued Miss Shaw's description to every police force in the country.'

'Why?' asked Carrington sourly. 'Do you expect her to be wandering the streets?'

'No sir, just a precaution.'

'I took the liberty of examining the things found on the bodies of those two dead men – the ones in the gravel pit. Look at this. A newspaper in a foreign language – Russian I think, or maybe Polish or Hungarian.'

The Doctor spoke without looking up. 'Anyone can buy a foreign newspaper, General.'

'And there's this comb,' said Carrington triumphantly. 'With a maker's imprint on it – in the same language.'

The Doctor stood up, took the comb from Carrington's hand, screwed a jeweller's glass into his eye and examined the minute writing. 'Tsk, tsk, very remiss of them, keeping this!'

'It could be a plant, sir,' said the Brigadier quietly.

Carrington waved the idea away. 'No, no, the only people capable of setting up a conspiracy like this are foreign agents with vast resources.'

'And hair-combs,' said the Doctor solemnly.

Carrington was quite sure his theory was correct.

'These people want to use the radiated astronauts as a weapon.'

'Your astronauts are still in orbit, General,' said the Doctor.

'Ridiculous!'

The Doctor waved a sheaf of notes in his face. 'When Professor Heldorf had the aliens in his care he recorded radio impulses.'

'Astronauts have radios in their helmets, Doctor.'

'Then why not use them to talk to Heldorf?' The Doctor headed for the door. 'I'm going to use the computer, Brigadier.' He turned to Carrington. 'I trust Taltallian won't hold a gun on me this time!'

'Nothing is to be gained by deciphering these impulses,' insisted Carrington. 'Your objective should be to find the astronauts.'

'My objective, General, is to find out what these aliens are trying to say to us.'

And with this parting shot, the Doctor strode from the room.

In the computer room the Doctor found Cornish and Taltallian discussing the problem of fuelling the recovery rocket. It appeared there was a shortage which could only be met by blending conventional fuel with the new and highly volatile M3 variant.

The Doctor entered and jabbed Taltallian in the back with a pencil. 'You're not armed, I hope?'

Taltallian half-raised his hands then lowered them as the Doctor took the pencil away and waved it at him. 'I would not have used the gun on a fellow scientist.'

'Have they found your assistant?' asked Cornish.

'Not yet,' said the Doctor briefly. 'May I use the computer?'

'Certainly. No doubt Doctor Taltallian will help

you. I'd like to see you about the rescue capsule. If you have a moment later?'

'Of course.'

Cornish left, and the Doctor said, 'Now, Doctor Taltallian, I'd like to programme in these impulse records . . .' He explained what he was attempting to do.

'This could take some considerable time, Doctor.'

'Well, it mustn't – '

The phone rang and Taltallian answered it. 'For you, Doctor.'

The Doctor took the receiver. 'Yes . . .' He listened, and his face hardened. 'Who is this?' The phone went dead and the Doctor hung up.

He looked hard at Taltallian. 'Someone's threatening to kill Miss Shaw . . . if I don't stop "interfering."'

The Doctor strolled over to the computer. 'Well, shall we get to work?'

Liz and Lennox, guarded by one of Reegan's thugs, were monitoring the progress of the three alien astronauts.

'Two million rads,' noted Liz. 'Dropping to two million minus fifty thousand . . .'

'Minus fifty thousand,' repeated Lennox, noting it down. He turned to the thug. 'You'd better let Reegan know there's only one more isotope left.'

The thug who was almost as slow-thinking as he was massive gave him a suspicious glare.

'Well?' said Lennox impatiently. 'Do you want them to die?'

'You'd better be right,' muttered the thug and went out of the main door at the top of the steps, locking it behind him.

Liz ran to the top of the steps and tried the door, but it wouldn't budge.

'No use,' said Lennox dully. 'They lock it.'

'Are you a prisoner too?'

'I can come and go as I please,' said Lennox, with a pathetic attempt at dignity. 'But I haven't anywhere to go'.

'You were a respected scientist once,' Liz reminded him.

'Grossly underpaid,' said Lennox bitterly.

He picked up a folded radiation suit. 'Can you help me, please?'

As Liz helped him into the suit, somehow a big metal key clattered onto the nearby lab table. 'I seem to have lost my key somewhere,' said Lennox casually.

As Liz helped him into the suit he whispered, 'They'll find me in the radiation chamber, understand? With the door locked from the outside.'

'Of course,' whispered Liz. 'Why not come with me?'

'Where would I go?'

Putting on his helmet Lennox opened the door to the radiation chamber. Liz locked it behind him, grabbed her coat and the key and ran for the door.

The Doctor studied the computer printout, provided by the somewhat unwilling help of Bruno Taltallian. 'Yes,' he muttered. 'I was right. These impulses are the mathematical formulae for building a machine.'

'What sort of a machine?' growled Taltallian.

'I shan't know that until I've built it.'

'You will defy the message threatening Miss Shaw's life?'

'How will these people know what I'm doing – unless someone tells them?'

'But who would do such a thing?'

'You, perhaps,' said the Doctor levelly. 'You've been consistently obstructive.'

Blusteringly, Bruno tried to defend himself. He had been acting under orders, it was monstrous that the Doctor should accuse him. 'Have you told the Brigadier of your suspicions?'

'I thought I might offer you an alternative,' said the Doctor. 'Instead of a ruthless grilling by the Brigadier, a few quiet words with me – and your name kept out of things.'

For a moment Taltallian looked tempted. Then he said hastily, 'I don't know what you're talking about.'

'I'll give you time to think about it,' said the Doctor cheerfully. 'Now, I must see what can be done about building this machine . . . Think about it, I'll expect to hear from you soon.'

When the Doctor had gone Bruno Taltallian stood quite still for a moment. Then he took a device like an advanced miniaturised walkie-talkie from his pocket, studied it, smiled and put it away again. Taking his coat and hat from a locker, he made for the door.

Liz emerged from the bunker and found that this laboratory like the former one was part of some kind of Government complex, though this one seemed run down and completely deserted.

Squeezing through rusting barbed wire, she ran down a rutted country lane. This led into a minor road, which in turn took her to a larger one, with cars zooming by.

After she had been travelling cross-country for quite a while she was feeling pretty exhausted. She decided to thumb a lift, not usually a difficult task for an attractive long-haired girl in a mini-skirt.

The first car sped straight by but to Liz's vast relief the second, a handsome Mercedes saloon, drew up beside her.

Then she recognised the driver. It was Bruno Taltallian, swathed in heavy overcoat and deerstalker, and once again he was holding a gun on her.

'Get in Miss Shaw,' said Taltallian.

Deciding that it just wasn't her day, Liz obeyed.

Soon afterwards Liz found herself back in the laboratory, trying to convince Reegan that the door had been left open and she'd escaped unaided. He was sceptical but unsure – the thug swore he'd locked the door but he was too dim to be relied on. Eventually he shoved Liz back towards Lennox with a snarled, 'Get back to work.' He turned to the thug. 'And you – make sure that door's kept locked.'

Thankfully Liz moved off, and Reegan looked at Taltallian. 'Well, did you bring it?'

Taltallian took the device from his pocket. With it he gave Reegan a printed list, explaining that it contained a communication code, a list of simple commands to give the alien astronauts. If they failed to obey, Reegan was to threaten to cut off their radiation supply – there was a signal for that as well.

'You will use these creatures to carry out a series of raids on carefully chosen targets,' concluded Taltallian. 'You know enough to do your job. Now, I have further instructions for you. Your call to the Doctor threatening Miss Shaw was stupid. It has merely made him more determined – and more suspicious of me. You must put him out of the way – permanently.'

'To save your neck?'

'He is on the point of discovering how to make one of these communication devices. He must be stopped.'

Reegan considered. 'All right, I'll deal with him.' He smiled. 'And since your own skin is in danger, you can help me . . .'

In the Brigadier's office, the Doctor and the Brigadier were drinking cups of army tea.

The Doctor had just finished describing his conversation with Taltallian. 'I think I rattled him,' he concluded.

'Surely Taltallian was only acting under Carrington's orders,' objected the Brigadier. 'Quinlan explained all that.'

'I heard him, and I didn't believe a word of it. They tried to keep us in the dark, and when that didn't work they fell back on a prepared cover story. Contagious radiation indeed!'

'Then what *is* happening?' demanded the Brigadier. 'An alien invasion – with Quinlan as a traitor?'

'I'll know that when I've built this machine, Brigadier.' The Doctor produced a long and complex list, and passed it over.

The Brigadier studied it dubiously. 'What's this?'

'Advanced electronic equipment. I need all of it – at once!'

The Brigadier winced, anticipating another savage bite from UNIT's budget. 'I'll see to it.'

'I suppose there's no news of Liz?' asked the Doctor hopefully.

'No, nothing. We're doing all we can, Doctor.'

'Yes, of course,' said the Doctor, and went on his way.

Liz and Lennox were working at a table close to the radiation chamber with Reegan's thug, now more morose and suspicious than ever, keeping guard.

'Thanks for keeping quiet,' whispered Lennox.

'Do you think he suspects?'

'Reegan suspects everyone,' said Lennox gloomily.

'If at first you don't succeed . . .'

'You won't get another chance,' muttered Lennox. 'How did they get you back so quickly anyway?'

'I ran into an old friend!'

Liz glanced at Taltallian who was waiting impatiently on the other side of the room, pacing up and down and glancing frequently and irritatedly at his watch.

At last Reegan came back, smiling broadly and clutching a small black attaché case, the kind high-powered ad-men carry documents in. 'Sorry about the delay – it's a delicate job.' He put the attaché case down on the table and opened it. 'It's perfectly simple, you just set the dial to the time-delay you need.' He pointed to a dial set into the lid. 'Now, how long will you need to get clear of the building?'

'Ten minutes, maybe more.'

'Say a quarter of an hour, then. Can't have you taking risks.' Setting the dial, Reegan snapped the case shut. 'Now, you leave the case as close to the Doctor as you can. Slide these catches *towards* each other' – Reegan mimed the action without actually doing it – 'and a quarter of an hour later – no more Doctor!'

'Suppose he tries to open the case when I've gone?'

'Same result a little earlier.'

'It's too risky,' muttered Taltallian.

Reegan smiled. 'It's you he's after.'

Taltallian nodded and turned away to put on his heavy coat. Reegan opened the case, re-adjusted the dial and closed it again.

By the time Taltallian turned round, the case was shut and Reegan was holding it out. 'There you are. Do as you're told, and your troubles will be over.'

Taltallian left, and from the other side of the long room Liz watched him go. The low-voiced conversation between the two men had been drowned by the deep hum of the laboratory generator, and Liz had no idea of the significance of the attaché case.

Fortunately for her peace of mind, she was quite unaware that she'd been witness to a plot against the Doctor's life . . .

'Every available astronaut is suddenly non-available,' said Cornish explosively. 'Not fit, transferred to other duties, awaiting security clearance.'

The Doctor smiled. 'My dear Controller, is that all?'

'All? What good's a recovery rocket without an astronaut?'

'I'll take the rocket up for you myself,' said the Doctor calmly.

'Doctor, I don't think you realise . . .'

'My dear fellow, I've spent more time in space than any astronaut on your staff. Not, I admit, in the rather primitive contraptions you use here, but I'll manage. I can also take considerably more g-force than most people, even though I do say so myself.'

'If you insist, Doctor. You'll have to take the tests . . .'

'Tests, simulations, anything you like. When that recovery capsule is ready, I'll take the rocket up.'

The door was flung open and the burly figure of Taltallian entered the computer room, bulkier than ever in his big tweed overcoat. He was carrying a small black attaché case with metal locks. In his big hands it looked like a toy.

At the sight of the Doctor, Taltallian stopped short. 'Ah, Doctor,' he cried, with uneasy heartiness, 'I was just coming over to see you.'

'Then I saved you a journey.'

Cornish said, 'Bruno, will you let me have those lift-off computations as soon as possible, please? Doctor, I'll go and set up those tests for you.'

As Cornish left, Bruno Taltallian came closer to the Doctor. 'I'll tell you everything,' he whispered. 'But you've got to give me a chance to get away.'

'Very well.'

'The information's in my car, I'll get it for you. You'll wait here?'

The Doctor looked curiously at him. 'All right.'

There was something very odd about all this, thought the Doctor. Why had Taltallian left the information in the car? Why was he so nervous, so insistent that the Doctor should stay right here?

Thoughtfully the Doctor wandered over to the computer and began studying the print-out.

Taltallian paused by the door. Turning, so that his body shielded the case from the Doctor's view, Taltallian pushed the catches towards each other.

At the sound of their click, everything came together in the Doctor's mind.

He hurled himself to the ground as the simultaneous thunder-clap and lightning flare of an explosion filled the computer room . . .

Somebody screamed . . .

10

'An Attack On The Space Centre?'

'I think I've got it now,' said Liz.

Reegan, who was no kind of scientist, had found the operation of Taltallian's communications device beyond him and had handed it over to Liz. Despite her worries, Liz found the task was a fascinating one.

'Send "stand up",' ordered Reegan.

Liz twisted the dial set into the device and pressed the transmitter button. The device gave out a low beeping sound – and the three figures in the radiation chamber rose slowly to their feet.

'Send "come forward".'

Liz made another adjustment, there was another low sound and the three figures began to advance towards the glass.

'Send "stop",' ordered Reegan hurriedly.

Liz obeyed and the figures stopped.

Reegan took the device from Liz and studied the call-sign list. 'I think I've got the hang of it. Nothing can go wrong?'

'It's simple enough; even you should be able to manage.' Liz paused. 'Taltallian brought you this thing, didn't he?

'Never you mind.'

'That case you gave him – what was that for?'

Reegan smiled. 'A way of killing two birds with one stone . . .'

The Brigadier and a somewhat dishevelled Doctor were watching a UNIT team sort and tidy the debris of the wrecked computer room.

'You seem to have been right about Taltallian, Doctor,' observed the Brigadier.

The Doctor brushed dust from his clothes and hair. 'Much good it did me – or him!'

'He was obviously trying to plant a time bomb on you. Lucky for you the mechanism was faulty.'

'I'm not so sure it was. Look at this.' The Doctor turned to a bench and picked up the twisted remnants of the bomb's timing mechanism. 'This was set at zero. Taltallian thought he had lots of time to get clear. But the bomb was set to explode straight away.'

'So whoever gave it to him wanted to get rid of both of you?'

'Yes,' said the Doctor thoughtfully. 'Taltallian was a bit of a weak link and his employers wanted to be rid of him. Luckily his body was between me and the bomb, so . . .' The Doctor waved towards Bruno's huddled body, as the UNIT stretcher-men began carrying it away.

'A dead end then?' said the Brigadier, with unconscious black humour.

'I'm afraid so . . .' The Doctor wandered over to Taltallian's locker. The door was hanging open, sprung loose by the blast, but the contents seemed undamaged.

The Doctor reached onto the top shelf and took out a small metal box with controls set in the lid.

'Brigadier, look at this.'

The Brigadier turned. 'What?'

'It's a communications device, very like the one I'm trying to build – and Taltallian had one all the time.'

'Time is running short,' said Quinlan pettishly. 'Cornish is nearly ready to send up that rocket.'

General Carrington said reproachfully, 'You were supposed to stop him, sir.'

'Do you think I haven't tried? I've tried every possible delay. Now, that Doctor's volunteered to pilot the recovery rocket.'

'He must be stopped!'

'We could tell him the truth,' suggested Quinlan.

'No! We know too little about him. He must be stopped. If that rocket goes up it means disaster for the entire world . . .'

After a low-voiced intense conversation, Reegan put down the phone and called to one of this henchmen, 'Will, go and bring the van round, there's a good fella.'

'Right you are, Mister Reegan.'

As the thug shambled off Lennox said, 'You're taking them away?'

'Just a short excursion. Open the door.'

Lennox opened the door to the radiation chamber and Reegan operated his newly-mastered device. One of the alien astronauts rose and marched towards the open door.

Reegan looked at Liz, tapping the device. 'Can this thing work the other way, so they can talk to me?'

Liz shook her head. 'No. All it does is send impulses they seem to understand.'

'But there could be a machine that would do that?'

'I imagine so.'

As the alien moved towards the door Reegan smiled. 'I think I'll be paying two visits tonight.'

The UNIT sentry at the gates of the Space Centre stared incredulously at the tall space-suited figure stalking towards him, its face invisible beneath the black glass of the helmet visor.

'Halt!' he called.

The figure marched on.

'Halt or I fire!'

The figure marched straight on, and the sentry drew his revolver. 'Halt or I fire' he repeated.

When the figure ignored him, he opened fire at point blank range, emptying the heavy service automatic into the astronaut's body, resting his arm on the crash barrier for a steady aim. The figure stalked on, unharmed and indeed unmarked by the hail of bullets.

It reached out and touched the barrier. A radiation surge flashed along the pole, sending the sentry's body crashing against his sentry-box, killing him instantly.

Unopposed, the alien strode on into the Centre.

A mixed group of UNIT soldiers and Space Centre technicians was hard at work repairing the wrecked computer room when the door swung open. They looked up in astonishment at the space-suited figure who stood in the doorway.

The nearest technician flung out a hand to bar the alien's advance. The second he touched it, radiation flared through his body, flinging him dead to the ground.

The others fled for the door, all except one UNIT soldier who tried to grapple with the intruder – and died the moment his fingers gripped its arm.

Seconds later the room was empty. The alien marched across to Taltallian's locker, looked inside, and then swept the contents of the shelf to the ground.

Another UNIT soldier appeared in the doorway, summoned by the fleeing technicians. He trained his rifle on the intruder and emptied the magazine into its body. He died instantly as the alien's hand brushed against his rifle barrel.

89

The alien stepped over the body and strode away.

Back in the Brigadier's office, he and the Doctor were examining the device found in Taltallian's locker.

'I tell you, it converts radio impulses into speech,' said the Doctor. 'The aliens in Heldorf's laboratory were trying to communicate with him.'

'So you were right, Doctor. They aren't human after all.'

'I never believed they were. Now, if only I can build the rest of this machine – '

'We could broadcast to the aliens?'

'Yes, probably. If you were to hurry up with those parts I've ordered . . .'

The Brigadier gave him a reproachful look. 'Most of them are coming from Japan, Doctor.' The phone rang and the Brigadier picked it up. 'Lethbridge-Stewart . . . Yes, he's here.' He passed the phone to the Doctor. 'It's Quinlan.'

'Yes, Minister?' said the Doctor.

'Doctor, I'd like to know if you still intend to pilot the recovery rocket?'

'Most certainly.'

'I can't persuade you that your action would be disastrous?'

'You might – if you were to tell me the whole truth.'

'You leave me no choice, Doctor. Will you come and see me please – at once?'

'Very well – and thank you, Minister.'

Putting down the phone the Doctor gave the Brigadier a quizzical look. 'He wants me to go and see him – says he'll tell me the whole truth.'

The Brigadier jumped up. 'I'll come with you, Doctor . . .'

The Doctor was already on his way. The Brigadier

was about to follow when the phone rang again. 'Yes, Lethbridge-Stewart . . . What? An attack on the Space Centre? Hang on!' The Brigadier looked up and called, 'Doctor, wait!' But the Doctor had gone. The Brigadier spoke into the phone. 'All right, all right. Calm down and tell me what's happened.'

Working in his Whitehall office, waiting for the Doctor, Quinlan looked up in irritation as the door opened – and shrank back in astonishment at the sight of a tall space-suited figure advancing towards him.

It laid a hand almost tenderly on his shoulder, and Quinlan's body glowed briefly with the radiation surge, and then slumped lifeless across his desk.

The alien turned and headed for an old-fashioned safe in the corner. A touch of its deadly hand blasted open the door, and another touch turned the papers in the safe to fiery ash.

Suddenly the door was flung open, obscuring the alien and the safe behind it. The Doctor paused for a moment, staring appalled at Quinlan's slumped body, then hurried forwards to the desk to examine it.

Satisfied that Quinlan was dead, the Doctor straightened up. The tall figure of the alien astronaut was stalking towards him, a gauntletted hand outstretched . . .

11

'Do You Really Think They're Not Human?'

Suddenly the Brigadier appeared in the doorway, his service automatic in his hand. He fired, and the alien swung round.

The Brigadier raised his weapon fired again. 'No, don't!' shouted the Doctor. 'Don't try to stop it – keep back!'

Lowering his automatic, the Brigadier stepped aside, and the alien, as if in response to some signal, started moving towards the door.

Unfortunately a UNIT soldier appeared and tried to bar the way. 'Keep back!' the Doctor shouted again, but it was too late.

The alien simply brushed the soldier aside, but the mere touch of its arm was fatal, and the soldier glowed and fell to the ground.

The alien moved through the doorway and closed the door. There was a flare of radiation at the handle, fusing the metal of the catch.

The Brigadier ran and tugged at it. 'Seems to be jammed.'

'There's no point in following it,' said the Doctor. 'There's nothing we can do.'

Lennox looked at the two aliens who were still in the radiation chamber. 'Do you really think they're not human?' he asked Liz.

'I intend to find out,' she said. 'Do you know where Reegan's taken the third one? Is Reegan in charge?'

'No. He works for someone, someone high-up.'

'He's got to be stopped.'

'You won't get away again.'

Liz looked hard at him. 'Maybe not. But you might . . .'

UNIT troops had arrived at Quinlan's office and broken open the jammed door. Quinlan's body had been taken away, and now the Doctor and the Brigadier were searching the debris for clues.

The Brigadier held out his hand. 'Look at these bullets, Doctor. Flattened.'

The Doctor examined them. 'Deflected by some kind of forcefield . . .'

'So there's no way of stopping them?'

'Not with bullets, Brigadier.'

A UNIT sergeant came into the room, saluted, and said, 'There's a strong radioactive trace as far as the road outside, sir. Then nothing.'

'Taken away in a vehicle,' said the Brigadier.

The Doctor nodded. 'Somebody's using these aliens, Brigadier. They're not free agents. They were brought to Earth for some purpose.'

'Conquest?' suggested the Brigadier.

'Perhaps . . . Or is that what we're supposed to think?'

In the control room of the Space Centre, the Doctor and Cornish were studying the plans for the forthcoming space flight.

'What's the rate of fuel consumption?' asked the Doctor.

'For the first two and a half minutes, fifteen tons per second.' Cornish hesitated, then said awkwardly. 'We'll have to use a mixture of standard fuel and the new M3 variant. We just can't get enough standard fuel in time.'

'Hasn't Quinlan's death made things easier?'

'Harder. Everything's wrapped up in red tape till they appoint a successor.'

Cornish picked up a file from his desk. 'Now, about your medical reports, Doctor, they really are rather incredible. According to this . . .'

'Yes, yes,' said the Doctor hurriedly. 'I told you it'd be all right . . .'

Guided by the device in Reegan's hand the alien astronaut lurched into the radiation chamber and collapsed, while its two fellows came close in silent concern.

At a barked order from Reegan, Lennox scrambled into a radiation suit, carried an isotope into the chamber and set it beside the unconscious alien, exposing the radioactive core.

Lennox came out and one of Reegan's thugs fastened the chamber door.

Liz looked at the collapsed astronaut. It was twitching feebly. 'What have you done to it?' she asked.

Reegan smiled. 'He's had a busy time.'

Lennox took off his helmet. 'Busy? Doing what?'

Reegan smiled even more broadly. 'Killing.'

'Who's been killed?' asked Liz.

'Some of your friends from UNIT.' Reegan was exultant. 'One touch from our friend in there and down they went. Bullets just bounce off them. With these three you could do anything. Walk into Fort Knox and help yourself.'

'And that's what you're going to do with them, is it?'

'I might,' said Reegan, and Liz could see he wasn't joking. He headed for the inner door. 'Lennox, keep feeding them radiation: I've a lot more work for them.'

He turned to the thug. 'Lock that main door and then come through to see me.'

As Reegan disappeared, and the thug moved to the door, Liz moved closer to Lennox and whispered, 'You're working for a murderer.'

'He was just boasting,' said Lennox uneasily.

'You don't really believe that.'

Lennox obviously didn't. 'Look, it's nothing to do with me, Miss Shaw,' he said. 'I'm just paid to look after them.'

'You're just as guilty as if you'd killed those people yourself!' she cried out. 'What are you going to do about it?'

'What can I do?' I'm too involved.'

'You can go to UNIT and tell them where we are.'

'Reegan would kill me.'

'Go to Brigadier Lethbridge-Stewart,' insisted Liz. 'He'll put you in protective custody.'

'I can't leave now,' protested Lennox. 'You left my key in the door, remember, and Reegan took it.'

Liz wasn't interested in excuses. 'Then you'll just have to talk your way out . . .'

General Carrington marched furiously into Cornish's control room. 'I understand you're going ahead with launching this rocket, Professor Cornish?'

'That's right.'

'I absolutely forbid it.'

'You haven't the authority to forbid it, General Carrington.'

'Why are you so against it?' asked the Doctor curiously.

Carrington began marching jerkily about the control room. 'Quinlan murdered, aliens attacking this Space Centre, the death of Doctor Taltallian . . . It's obviously just the beginning.'

'The beginning of what?'

'An alien invasion, Doctor, with the collaboration of some foreign power.'

The Doctor shook his head, astonished at the way Carrington was fitting the facts to his theory.

'All the more reason for me to go up in that rocket and find out what's happened up there.'

Carrington swung round on the Doctor. 'Are you a trained astronaut, sir?'

Cornish said impatiently, 'He's perfectly capable of making the trip – '

Carrington interrupted him. 'You haven't answered my question, Doctor.'

'And you haven't answered mind, General,' countered the Doctor. 'Why are you so opposed to this launch?'

Suddenly Carrington changed tack. 'Professor Cornish, could that rocket carry a nuclear warhead?'

'Yes,' said Cornish reluctantly.

'Then that is what it *should* be used for.'

The Doctor sighed. 'Since we don't know what's up there, isn't it more sensible to send a man rather than a bomb?'

After a few more futile exchanges, Carrington turned and headed for the door. 'I shall go to the highest authority to have you stopped.'

Cornish had reached the end of his patience. 'Then you'd better get on with it, General. We blast off in two hours time . . .'

Lennox watched through the window of the radiation chamber as the third alien astronaut struggled back to its feet. 'It's recovering!'

But Liz was relentless. 'So Reegan can use it to

commit more murders. You'll have to get a message out.'

'That's impossible.'

'Here's the telephone,' said Liz, pointing. 'You're allowed to use it.'

'All the calls are monitored.'

The main door opened and Reegan's thug Tony came in, locking it behind him. He sat down in his usual chair and picked up his newspaper.

Liz moved closer to Lennox and whispered, 'Demand to see Reegan. Say the isotopes are running low.'

'He'll never believe me.'

'*Try*!' hissed Liz.

Lennox braced himself and walked round to stand in front of Tony's chair. 'I want to see Mister Reegan. It's urgent.'

'It'll have to wait. He's gone to London. Meeting with the boss.'

Lennox sighed and was about to give up, when Liz stepped forward. She pointed to the aliens. 'They're dying in there. Look at those readings, you can see for yourself.'

Tony peered at the dials on the monitoring consoles, though it was clear they meant nothing to him.

Lennox pointed to a dial. 'Look, that one reads minimum. It should be at maximum. We're running out of isotopes. I've got to go and get more . . .'

It took quite a lot more arguing and persuasion before Tony was convinced that it was all right for Lennox to go, but finally he unlocked the door and let him out, locking it again behind him.

He came back and looked worriedly at the dials, then suspiciously at Liz. He peered through the window at the aliens and muttered, 'They don't look as if they're dying to me . . .'

Liz managed to hide her smile.

Controller Cornish ran through a last series of checks then turned to the Doctor. 'Time you were in the preparation room, Doctor.'

'All right, I'm on my way.'

The Brigadier had come to see his old friend off. 'Why have they advanced the blast-off time?' he asked.

'There seems to be some opposition to my going. General Carrington wants to cancel the launch.'

A loudspeaker voice called: 'Astronaut to Preparation Chamber at once please.'

'Right,' said the Doctor briskly. 'I must be off.'

A technician handed the Brigadier a phone. 'There's a call for you sir.'

Sergeant Benton was on the line. 'A man called Lennox has turned up out of the blue, sir. Very frightened. Says he knows something about the missing astronauts, and he'll only talk to you in person. Wants us to put him in protective custody.'

The Brigadier considered. 'Better put him in a cell, Benton,' he said. 'Tell him I'll be back as soon as possible.'

Sergeant Benton showed the terrified Lennox along a corridor and opened the heavy metal door at the end.

Lennox looked at the little cell in alarm. 'You're putting me in here?'

'You asked for protective custody, sir. Can't be safer than in a cell.'

Lennox pointed to the barred semi-circular window set high in the wall. 'What's out there?'

'Just a yard, sir,' said Benton soothingly. 'What are you so frightened about?'

'I can only tell the Brigadier. Will he be long?'

'He'll be back as soon as he can, sir. Shall I get you a cuppa?'

Lennox shook his head. 'No thanks, I'm all right. You will lock the door, won't you?'

'Yes sir,' said Benton patiently.

Thinking that this must be the most unusual prisoner he'd ever had, he went out and locked the door behind him.

'Report on astronaut readiness,' requested Cornish.

'Astronaut now proceeding through quarantine area to capsule . . .'

The Brigadier stood waiting in a bare metal room, ornamented with a vaguely arty-looking abstract mural, a couch and a potted plant. He supposed it must be a kind of astronaut's ante-room.

The door opened and the Doctor entered, resplendent in full astronaut gear, carrying the helmet under his arm. 'Hello, Brigadier, what are you doing here?'

'Thought I'd see you off, Doctor. They said I could wait here.'

The Doctor looked round the room. 'Not very impressive for one's last sight of Earth, is it?'

A voice came from a hidden speaker: 'Astronaut to capsule please.'

The Doctor held out his hand. 'Goodbye, Brigadier.'

'Goodbye, Doctor – and good luck.'

A lift door opened on the far side of the room, and the Doctor entered the little cabin that would carry him to the summit of the great gantry, where the capsule waited on top of the massive rocket.

The doors began to close, and the Doctor gave a cheery wave and disappeared from view. The Brigadier looked at the closed lift doors for a moment, then turned and went back the way he had come.

12

'Large Unidentified Object Approaching On Collision Course . . .'

Reegan had just returned to the bunker laboratory to find that Lennox has disappeared. He was not pleased about it.

After demolishing the excuses of this terrified thug, he turned on Liz. 'You put Lennox up to this.' He gestured at the three shapes behind the window. 'There's nothing wrong with them.'

Liz stuck to her story. 'We thought they were dying . . .'

'Nonsense! The readings haven't changed since I left. Where's he gone?'

'I told you – to get more isotopes.' Suddenly Reegan produced a gun. He jammed it under Liz's chin, forcing her head back. 'You're lying. Did you send him to see your friends at UNIT? Is that it? *Answer me!*'

Choking, Liz twisted her head away from the gun. 'All right, he's gone to Lethbridge-Stewart at UNIT. You're too late.'

Reegan flung her across the room. 'Don't you believe it!' He snatched up the phone. 'Give me the direct emergency line . . . Listen, we're in trouble, Lennox has gone to UNIT . . .'

He paused, listening to the instructions from the other end, then smiled. 'Right, you take care of Lennox and I'll deal with the Doctor.'

'Control to capsule,' said Cornish. 'Have you completed your instrument check?'

The Doctor, strapped in the capsule's tiny control

cabin, flicked a casual glance around the battery of instruments in front of him and said just as casually, 'Yes, it all seems to be working all right.'

There was a pause, then Cornish's voice came back, translating the Doctor's reply into the correct jargon. 'Capsule reports instrument systems at go.'

The Doctor sighed. 'How much longer have I got to wait in here?' he asked impatiently.

'We are at zero minus thirty-three minutes.'

I take it you mean about half an hour. How's the fuel situation?'

'Fifty-five per cent conventional fuel on board. Switching to M3 variant at sixty-five per cent.'

Delay was making the Doctor tetchy. 'Can't you hurry it up? It's very boring sitting here.'

'We can't hurry the M3 variant, Doctor, it's highly volatile.

'I still think you ought to put in a higher proportion of M3,' said the Doctor argumentatively. 'The extra g-force wouldn't worry me.'

It would worry you if the rocket blew up on lift-off, Doctor,' said Cornish drily. 'I'm not taking the chance.'

The Space Centre Fuel Bay was an area of storage tanks and tangled piping just to one side of the launch area. A bored UNIT sentry was patrolling the area when he saw a jaunty figure in overall and baseball cap, carrying a tool bag and whistling cheerfully, come strolling towards him.

'Oy, where do you think you're going?'

'They need me in Fuel Control,' said the man cheerfully. 'There's been a bit of a breakdown.'

'News to me,' said the sentry suspiciously. 'Where's your pass?'

The man fished a piece of paper from his pocket and

held it out. By the time the sentry had registered it was just a crumpled envelope, a savage two-finger jab to the solar plexus had doubled him up, and a slashing chop to the side of the neck had laid him out.

Catching the body over his shoulder as it fell, Reegan hoisted it up and dumped it out of sight behind a fuel bunker. Then he ran up a metal ladder and along the catwalk that ran alongside the rows of fuel storage tanks.

A technician was working on a connecting line just ahead. He heard Reegan coming towards him, looked up and tried to grapple with him. Reegan lifted his leg and booted the man over the edge. Peering down at the motionless body below for a moment, Reegan went on his way.

At last he reached his destination, the junction point that connected the tanks of the new M3 variant, a fuel as powerful as it was unstable, to the supply of regular fuel.

Glancing up at the towering silver shape of the rocket just beyond the fuel bays, Reegan took a wrench from his tool bag and began closing a connecting tap . . .

Suddenly a loudspeaker voice rang through the control room: 'Emergency, emergency! Fuel injection malfunction . . .'

'Control to fuel bay,' snapped Cornish. 'Check all fuel injection circuits!'

The Doctor's irritable voice came over the intercom. 'Now what?'

'Temporary fuel injection malfunction, Doctor. We're checking it out.'

Almost immediately the voice said, 'Fuel injection systems functioning normally.'

'It's all right, Doctor,' said Cornish. 'The fault's self-rectified.'

Reegan finished opening a turncock and stepped back with a smile of satisfaction.

Fuel was flooding into the Doctor's rocket once more. But thanks to Reegan's efforts it was the new M3 variant – much sooner and in much greater quantity than Cornish had ever planned.

Reegan was still smiling as he walked away. According to his information, there was a very good chance that the rocket would blow up on take-off. Failing that, it would blast off at such a rate that the Doctor would be instantly killed by the increased g-force.

The technicians at Space Control would be sending a corpse into space.

Stretched out half-dozing on his bunk, Lennox woke with a start when the door opened and a uniformed figure entered the cell, carrying a tray which was covered with a domed metal dish-cover.

The soldier put the tray down on the little table. 'I've brought you some food.' He lifted the big dome, revealing a smaller one. Lennox rubbed his eyes, 'Thanks. You'll lock the door again won't you?'

'Oh yes,' said the soldier. 'I'll lock the door.'

Reassured, Lennox heard the door slam and the key turn in the lock outside.

He was feeling quite hungry he realised, as he lifted the metal plate cover . . .

He was looking at his death.

An unshielded radioactive isotope lay on the plate . . . Lennox backed away, huddling into the corner of his cell. He stared at the gleaming metal cylinder in front of him, and knew he was already dead . . .

The Brigadier drove his Land-rover into the fuel bay area. He was making a check of his sentries.

He frowned, realising that the fuel bay sentry was not at his post. Stopping the Land-rover, the Brigadier looked round – and saw the missing sentry staggering towards him. Jumping out of the Land-rover he ran towards him. 'What happened, man?'

'Someone dressed as . . . mechanic,' gasped the soldier. 'Hit me . . . He was heading for . . . M3 storage tanks . . .'

The Brigadier helped the sentry into the back of his Land-rover and drove back towards Space Control at top speed . . .

'We're all set, Doctor,' announced Cornish. 'Lift-off fifteen seconds.' He glanced at his monitor screen, which showed the silver needle of the rocket, ready to blast off.

In the control cabin of the capsule the Doctor stretched and relaxed. 'About time too . . .'

'All right,' said Cornish quietly. 'Final countdown-now.' His level voice began marking off the seconds. Ten . . . nine . . . eight . . . seven . . . six . . . five . . . four . . . three . . .'

The Brigadier clattered into Space Control. 'Stop the countdown! Controller, you must stop lift-off!'

'Two . . . one . . . zero,' completed Cornish. 'It's too late Brigadier . . .'

On the monitor the silver needle was rising on a pillar of fire . . . rising much too fast.

'We have lift-off,' announced a loudspeaker voice.

104

A second, panicky voice came seconds later. 'Lift-off speed twenty per cent in excess and rising . . .'

'There's been some kind of sabotage in the fuel bay!' shouted the Brigadier.

Cornish was intent on the rocket. 'Reduce fuel burn rate.'

A report came back: 'Fuel burn rate will not reduce. Computer calculates fuel burn indicates forty-eight per cent M3 variant . . .'

'Forty-eight per cent!' Cornish was appalled.

The Brigadier leaned forward. 'What will happen?'

At over twenty per cent in excess of planned lift-off speed he'll blow himself out of Earth's orbit and go into the sun . . . Reduce flame apertures!'

At a nearby console a technician studied her instrument-readings. 'Flame apertures will not reduce, owing to excess heat.'

Cornish spoke into his mike. 'Doctor, can you operate manual control on flame apertures? You must reduce speed. Doctor, do you read me?'

The Doctor's distorted voice came back. 'I can . . . hear . . . you . . . g-force too . . . great.

Cornish flicked a switch and the Doctor appeared on the screen. His whole face was distorted by the incredible pressure of gravity.

'Doctor, can you operate manual control?'

'I'll . . . try . . .'

They saw the Doctor lean forward, fighting against the enormous pressure of gravity. With a mighty effort he operated controls on the console before him.

'Are the controls responding?' asked Cornish tensely.

'No . . . must be . . . excess heat,' said the Doctor. 'Can . . . you . . . jettison . . . stage one . . . prematurely?'

'If we do that you may never go into orbit at all.'

'If we jettison . . . stage one . . . now . . . chance the excess momentum . . . will bring me into . . . orbit!'

'It's a very slim chance, Doctor.'

'Better than orbit . . . round sun! Please jettison . . . stage one . . . now!'

'Jettison stage one now,' ordered Cornish.

'Stage one jettisoned.'

'Radar report – stage one exploded immediately after separation. Speed now reducing to normal.'

The Doctor's voice came through clear and strong: 'I'm very much obliged to you, Professor Cornish. That seems to have done it . . . What went wrong?'

'Sabotage, Doctor. Too much M3 variant in your fuel.'

'They're very persistent, aren't they?' said the Doctor grimly.

'Stage two, fifteen seconds to separation,' announced a technician's voice. There was a brief pause and then a second announcement. 'Stage two jettisoned.'

Cornish sat back, relaxing a little. He turned to the Brigadier. 'A thirty-second burn on stage three rockets and he'll be in orbit!'

It was some time later and things were quiet in the control room.

The dangerous first stage of his journey over, the Doctor was moving steadily towards his objective.

'Control to capsule,' said Cornish, 'do you have visual contact yet?'

In the capsule control cabin, the Doctor peered out through the viewing port. 'If you mean can I see it, the answer's no.'

Cornish's patient voice came back. 'You are within half a mile of Mars Probe Seven and converging.

Change attitude of capsule three degrees. Doctor, change attitude of capsule three degrees – now.'

'All right, all right, Mister Cornish,' grumbled the Doctor. 'More haste less speed.'

The Doctor adjusted controls, the capsule tilted and he gazed out of the viewing port again – and there was Mars Probe Seven hanging in space, looking incredibly close.

'I can see it now. Manoeuvring for link-up . . .'

In the control room of the Space Centre they watched tensely as the Doctor carried out the delicate link-up with masterly precision.

His voice came through again. 'I'm going through into Mars Probe Seven now.'

'Careful Doctor,' warned Cornish. 'We don't know what's in there.'

'Of course we do,' said the Doctor briskly. 'Your three astronauts are in there. I'm just going to inject air into the tunnel . . .'

On the screen in space control they watched the Doctor rise and drift gently across the cabin.

Suddenly the voice of the radar technician rang through the control room. 'Large unidentified object, converging with Mars Probe Seven on collision course. Estimated speed seven thousand miles per hour, decreasing . . .'

Cornish leaned forward urgently. 'Doctor, large unidentified object approaching on collision course. Take evasive action! Take evasive action!'

In the cabin of the capsule, the Doctor looked out of the viewing port.

An immense glowing sphere was rushing straight towards him.

13

'The Capsule Will Be Smashed To Fragments . . .'

Too fascinated to be afraid, the Doctor studied the approaching sphere.

It glowed so fiercely that the Doctor was unable to make out much detail. It seemed to be a sort of flattened sphere, rather like an amoeba, with some kind of darker inner core.

The glowing surface resembled nothing the Doctor had ever seen before. It was as though the approaching ship was somehow made of light . . .

Cornish's agitated voice came over the intercom. 'What is it, Doctor? Can you see?'

'Some kind of spaceship. It's enormous . . .'

'Can you evade it?'

Recalled to the realities of the situation, the Doctor said, 'I can try!'

Kicking off against the wall, he boosted himself back into the control chair.

The Brigadier and Cornish were watching the big radar screen, where they could see two dots, one large, one small. The larger dot was moving ever closer to the smaller one.

'He hasn't got the speed,' murmured the Brigadier.

Cornish nodded. 'He's still linked to Mars Probe Seven.'

'How much fuel has he got for manoeuvring?'

'Precious little,' said Cornish ruefully. 'He'll need all of it for re-entry.'

They saw the Doctor frantically operating controls

and heard his distorted voice: 'It's closing in too fast. I can't – '

On the radar screen, the large dot swallowed the smaller. In the same instant, the Doctor's voice cut off and the monitor screen went blank.

'They must have collided,' said the Brigadier. 'What's happened to him?'

'If they *have* collided,' said Cornish grimly, 'The capsule will be smashed to fragments . . .'

The huge alien vessel didn't so much collide with the Doctor's capsule as absorb it.

There was a sort of silent shuddering sensation that knocked the Doctor unconscious. When he awoke he was still in his control chair, apparently unharmed.

A deep, throaty voice boomed out, '*You are not in danger.*'

'Where am I?'

'*Your vessel is on board our spacecraft. Open your hatch and leave the capsule.*'

The Doctor rose, noticing that something very close to Earth gravity was in operation. 'Very well. What has happened to our three astronauts?'

'*They are unharmed. Open the hatch and leave the capsule.*'

The Doctor reached for his space helmet.

'*You will not need life support systems. An environment has been prepared.*'

Rising from his chair, the Doctor went to the exterior hatch and began unscrewing the locking wheel. If the hatch opened on to space he would be dead in seconds, he thought. But then, if his captors wanted him dead, he'd be dead already.

He swung the hatch open and climbed out. He was standing in a tunnel of light.

Cautiously, the Doctor moved along the tunnel. Somehow he seemed to be floating rather than walking . . . There was some kind of door at the end of the tunnel. It slid open as he approached.

The Doctor went through the door and found himself in a room. It was a very familiar looking room – bare metal walls, an arty looking abstract mural, a potted plant . . . Suddenly the Doctor realised. It was very like the astronaut departure lounge in which he'd said goodbye to the Brigadier.

In the centre of the room was a circular device with a built-in screen. It was clearly some kind of television set. A pattern of swirling lights was filling the screen and three men sat grouped round it, staring in apparent fascination. They were talking animatedly, all more or less at once.

'Look at that – it was an open goal!'

'He had all the time in the world, why didn't he shoot? *I* could have scored then!'

'You ought to be playing, then!'

'Don't need to, do I? We're a goal ahead . . .'

The Doctor recognised all three men immediately. He had studied their files back at the Space Centre. The stocky fair-haired one was Charles Van Leyden. The others, one small and dark, the other beaky-nosed and thin, were Frank Michaels and Joe Lefee, the two men Van Leyden had come to rescue.

Lefee glanced up as the Doctor entered. 'Hello, come in.' He swung round in his chair. 'Do you happen to know how long we're being kept here?'

'You're missing the match,' called Michaels.

The Doctor stared at the swirling light patterns on the screen.

'Never mind,' snapped Lefee. 'Turn it off.'

Grumbling, Michaels obeyed.

'Any idea when we'll see our families?' Van Leyden

asked the Doctor.

The Doctor looked around at the three cheerful faces. 'Where do you think you are?' he asked.

Van Leyden chuckled. '*You* ought to know.'

'Please, answer me. Do you know where you are?'

'Yes, of course. I brought these two fellows back from Mars Probe Seven and they slapped us all in extended quarantine.'

'So you think you're on Earth – at the Space Centre?'

Lefee pointed to the window – which was covered by a dull metal screen. 'What do you think that is?'

Michaels jumped up. 'Just what do you want?'

'I came to take you all back to Earth.'

There was a burst of laughter.

'*Back* to Earth?' asked Van Leyden incredulously.

'Who let him in?' demanded Lefee.

'Listen to me, gentlemen,' said the Doctor urgently. 'You're not on Earth, nor are you at the Space Centre. You're prisoners on an alien spaceship!' He turned to Van Leyden. 'You came up here in Recovery Seven, but you never made the journey back. Something happened. Try to remember . . .'

Van Leyden stared hard at him, something coming to life in his eyes. 'Yes . . . something happened.'

A sustained electronic chord vibrated through the room, and the screen lit up again, though no one had touched it. The three men turned away as one, sat down in their respective chairs and stared at the swirling light pattern.

The Doctor waved his hand before Van Leyden's eyes, but the man didn't even blink. He did the same thing to Michaels, and snapped his fingers under Lefee's nose.

There was no reaction.

'Van Leyden! Michaels! Lefee!' called the Doctor.

A voice from behind him said, '*They cannot hear you.*'

111

The Doctor spun round. The wall behind him had become semi-transparent and behind it he could make out the outline of a tall shape, standing by a machine. It was humanoid, with a body, a head, arms and legs – but it wasn't human.

The huge round head had a corrugated sheen and its only discernible features were two fiercely glowing eyes. The Doctor waved towards the frozen astronauts and said indignantly, 'You've conditioned their minds!'

'*It was necessary to preserve their health. Their condition was deteriorating.*'

'Why make them prisoners in the first place?'

'*Why have you not returned our ambassadors?*'

'Ambassadors?'

'*An agreement was made – a treaty. You have betrayed us.*'

'Ambassadors!' said the Doctor again. Suddenly he was beginning to understand a great deal . . .

Carrington arrived in the control room to find Cornish and the Brigadier listening to a report from the computer section.

'Radio telescope report from Jodrell Bank. Computer analysis estimates object to be discoid in shape, half a mile in diameter.'

'Half a mile?' The Brigadier was astonished. 'It must be a meteor.'

Cornish glanced at the giant radar screen. The larger dot was still in exactly the place it had occupied when it swallowed the dot that represented the Doctor's capsule. 'Meteors don't stand still,' he remarked thoughtfully.

'It's obviously an alien spacecraft,' snapped Carrington. 'We must attack and destroy it.'

'What about the Doctor, sir?' protested the Brigadier. 'If that thing is a spacecraft he may be on board.'

'He must be dead by now,' said Carrington dismissively. 'We must send up a rocket with an atomic warhead.'

There was something different about General Carrington, thought the Brigadier. The diffident courtesy was gone and his whole manner was harsh and abrupt, almost dictatorial.

'Until we know for certain . . .' began Cornish.

Carrington cut him off. 'We *do* know!' He turned towards the door. 'I must go. There's a meeting of the Security Council in an hour's time. This object has been spotted all over the world.'

'What are you going to say to the Council, sir?' asked the Brigadier.

'I shall recommend an immediate, all-out attack. We must defend ourselves while there is still time.' Carrington turned and marched briskly off.

Cornish shook his head despairingly. 'The man's mad!'

'Not necessarily,' said the Brigadier thoughtfully. 'I've a feeling General Carrington knows more than he's telling us. He was on Mars Probe Six, remember. Perhaps he discovered something . . .'

'Are you supporting his plan – just to attack blindly?'

The Brigadier shook his head. 'No. I think we should wait. Our only hope is that the Doctor is still alive.'

'What you have been telling me is appalling,' said the Doctor. 'I can assure you the authorities on Earth had no knowledge of this dreadful business.'

'*That is difficult to believe.*'

113

'I can assure you it's the truth. Let me go back to Earth and I will personally ensure that your ambassadors are returned safely.'

'*Do you know where they are?*'

'With the information you've given me I can soon find out. You must let me try.'

For a long time the alien shape was silent, as if considering the matter. Then it said: '*Very well – but remember, If our ambassadors are not soon returned, we shall destroy the Earth.*'

The very matter-of-factness of the threat made it all the more believable.

The Doctor indicated the three hypnotised astronauts. 'May I take these men back with me?'

'*No. They will remain here until our ambassadors are returned. You may return to your capsule.*'

The wall became solid again. The pattern on the screen changed and suddenly the astronauts were conscious again.

Van Leyden looked at the Doctor. 'Something happened . . .'

'Don't worry,' said the Doctor cheerfully. 'I'm going to get you out of this quarantine soon.'

'The sooner the better,' grumbled Lefee.

'Send us in something to read, will you?' asked Michaels.

'Yes, yes,' said the Doctor vaguely. 'Don't worry, I'll see to everything.'

The sliding door opened, and the Doctor walked off down the long tunnel of light to the waiting capsule. As soon as the door closed behind him, the three men forgot his existence.

Lefee leaned forwards and touched a control on the television device. 'We might just catch the end of the game . . .'

14

'Your Doctor Friend Is As Dead As A Doornail . . .'

The Brigadier came back into the control room after a brief visit to UNIT HQ, where he had hoped to interrogate a prisoner. 'Anything happening?' he asked.

Cornish looked up. 'The Americans are planning to send up an unmanned capsule to observe the alien vessel. What about this prisoner of yours, this man Lennox? Did he tell you anything?'

For a moment the Brigadier didn't reply. Then he said bitterly, 'No. He was murdered – in his cell.'

'In your own headquarters?'

'Someone put an isotope in with him.'

'You're not having a great deal of success, are you, Brigadier? The astronauts still missing, Miss Shaw kidnapped, now Lennox murdered under your nose.'

'We've identified the two radioactive bodies found in that gravel pit,' said the Brigadier defensively. 'They certainly weren't foreign agents – they were petty criminals from London. The explosive that killed Taltallian has been identified too – the new H37 compound, not even issued to the Army yet.'

'So our own people could be involved?'

'That was always the Doctor's theory . . .' The Brigadier described UNIT's efforts to track down an insecticide in the mud on Lennox's boots and the source of the isotope in his cell, both so far unsuccessful.

Cornish nodded, 'You've been very thorough.'

'Yes,' said the Brigadier savagely. 'But it doesn't seem to have got me anywhere.'

Suddenly the Doctor's face was on the monitor

screen again and his cheerful voice filled the control room. 'Hello, Space Control, can you read me?'

Cornish sat bolt upright in his chair. 'Control to Recovery Seven, we read you loud and clear.'

'Doctor!' called the Brigadier joyfully. 'Are you all right?'

'Yes, thank you, Brigadier.'

'Have you found my astronauts?' asked Cornish urgently.

'Yes, they're safe and sound. I can't tell you any more now, it isn't safe. I shall maintain radio silence until re-entry. Brigadier, put your men on standby. I'll tell you everything when I land.'

'What has happened to my astronauts? Control to Recovery Seven, do you read me?'

They saw the Doctor lean forward and flick a switch, and everything went silent.

The Brigadier smiled. 'It's no good, he won't talk till he wants to. I must get on to my HQ.'

The Brigadier hurried off, happy that the Doctor was alive and well and on his way back, and that somehow things were moving.

'This is Control,' said Cornish. 'Recovery Seven is now approaching re-entry orbit . . .'

Swaddled in a protective suit several sizes too big for her, Liz Shaw knelt in the radiation chamber, carefully raising the radioactive central core of an isotope from its encasing metal cylinder.

In Lennox's absence, the task of caring for the alien astronauts had devolved onto her. Somehow she felt a responsibility towards them.

As she rose to leave, one of the aliens barred her way. Liz waited, apprehensively.

Then to her amazement the alien raised gauntleted

hands to his helmet and lifted it slowly from his head.

Liz gave a gasp of horror and backed away. The face revealed was somehow blurred and glowing, difficult to focus the eyes upon. It had a lumpy, corrugated unfinished look, like a head crudely modelled from rough clay, and the features were rudimentary, apart from the deep-set burning eyes.

The alien stood looking at Liz for a moment. It raised a hand almost in appeal and took a step towards her. Liz turned and fled and Lennox's thug locked the door of the radiation chamber.

Reegan, returning from another of his mysterious errands came briskly down the steps, shrugging off his trench-coat. He found Liz leaning against an instrument console visibly shaken. 'What's the matter with you?' he asked.

'Look!' Liz pointed to the helmetless alien who was standing close to the big glass window.

Even Reegan was a little taken aback, though he tried not to show it. 'Ugly looking feller, isn't he?'

'You knew they weren't human?'

'I had a pretty good idea.'

'Why did you bring them here, then?'

'I was paid.'

'Who by?'

'Never you mind,' said Reegan thoughtfully. 'I've got some ideas of my own now.'

'Like robbing Fort Knox?'

Reegan nodded cheerfully. 'Or the Bank of England . . . or anywhere!'

'And is that what your employer wants?'

'Doesn't matter what he wants – we've got them.'

'We?'

'There's a vacancy. Lennox had a little accident at UNIT HQ.'

'You killed him!' accused Liz.

'Never laid a finger on him,' said Reegan truthfully. 'Well, what about it?'

Liz was incredulous. 'Are you offering me a job?'

'What do you say?'

'What's the alternative?' asked Liz cautiously.

'I kill you and buy myself another scientist – ' The shrill of the telephone interrupted him. 'Think about it,' he advised her, and picked up the receiver.

'Reegan,' he spoke into the receiver. 'Oh, it's you, sir . . .' He listened for some time then said, 'So the Doctor's on his way down? I did my best to stop him going up . . .' Another pause. 'I see. Are you sure you want him dead? He might come in useful. All right, all right, I'll see to it.'

He put down the phone. 'Your friend the Doctor is on his way back from a little trip. I'm going to be his reception committee . . .'

The Brigadier stood watching in the control room as the Doctor went through landing procedures with his usual skill.

'Capsule drifting on course,' said a loudspeaker voice. 'No rectification needed.'

'How long before he's down?' asked the Brigadier.

'Four point five minutes,' said Cornish precisely. 'He's making a perfect descent, right on the touchdown pad.'

'I'll go and meet him.'

As the Brigadier hurried away Cornish called. 'He'll have to go through decontamination first.'

'How long will that take?'

'Under an hour.'

'An hour!'

'Think yourself lucky, Brigadier. It used to take two weeks . . .'

Reegans' van – it was a bakery van today – drove up to a side entrance of the sprawling complex of Space HQ. This time Reegan wasn't leaving any tell-tale bodies behind him. Somehow he had obtained all the necessary passes to admit him to the Space Centre's de-contamination area.

Consulting a map on the dashboard, Reegan drove to a precise point in the decontamination area and parked the van. Jumping out, he stripped off his white coat to reveal a technician's overalls and took a long coil of plastic hose and a gas cylinder from the back of the van.

Reegan headed for a particular junction point in the tangle of pipes that made up the ventilation system . . .

'Astronaut now entering decontamination area,' announced the loudspeaker voice.

Cornish looked up at the Brigadier, who was hovering impatiently by the door. 'Relax, Brigadier, he won't be long now . . .'

Wearing a somewhat gaudily-shaped dressing gown, the Doctor came out of the shower area and into the astronaut dressing room. He was pleased to see his own clothes, neatly cleaned and pressed, awaiting him on hangers.

Whistling cheerfully, the Doctor started to get dressed.

(Reegan, meanwhile was working at frantic speed, fitting an adaptor he had taken from his pocket to the ventilation system and connecting that, by means of the plastic hose, to his cylinder of gas . . .)

Slipping into his jacket the Doctor hung his borrowed dressing gown on a hanger and spoke into a mike set close to the closed door. 'Right, I'm ready when you are.'

Cornish's voice came back over the speaker. 'Just a few minutes more, Doctor, we're waiting for final test results.'

'Anything you say, Mister Cornish,' said the Doctor agreeably, and sat down on the metal bench. They might have provided a few dog-eared copies of *Punch*, he thought. Even the captured human astronauts had had their hypnotic TV set . . .

Bored, the Doctor stretched out flat on the long bench, ready for a little doze.

(Reegan finished his work and swung the opening-wheel on the gas cylinder. There was the faintest of hisses as the gas flooded into the ventilation system.)

The Doctor became aware of a strange, acrid, choking smell. He coughed, and the cough turned into a coughing fit. Sitting up, he became aware of white smoke seeping from one of the ventilator grilles.

The Doctor got up and took a step forward. He had to reach the intercom, call for help . . .

He took a couple of uncertain steps forward, then collapsed . . .

Reegan stood listening to the flow of gas, checking off the seconds on his watch.

A couple of seconds more and then he shut off the gas, slipped on a protective plastic mask that he took from his pocket, and headed for the decontamination building. He found his way to the decontamination suite without trouble, and opened the door.

The Doctor lay huddled on the floor in the centre of the room. Reegan went over to the body, and putting forth all his considerable strength, hoisted the Doctor over his shoulder and carried him from the room.

'Decontamination Section report. All tests satisfactory.' Cornish spoke into his console mike. 'All right. You've cleared, Doctor.'

There was no reply.

'Doctor, do you read me?'

Still nothing.

'I'm going over there,' said the Brigadier urgently and hurried away.

Reegan's baker's van was speeding towards the entrance . . .

. . . just as the Brigadier burst into the gas-filled room. Covering nose and mouth as best he could with his handkerchief, the Brigadier staggered over to the intercom. 'Cornish, the Doctor's gone . . . there's gas in here. Seal off all the gates.'

Reegan drove up to the UNIT checkpoint by which he'd entered, showed his pass and gave the sentry a cheerful wave.

The sentry inspected the pass, returned the wave and lifted the barrier. Reegan drove through, just as the telephone in the checkpoint's sentry box started to ring . . .

General Carrington received the news of the Doctor's disappearance with a mixture of scepticism and rage. He seemed to be of the opinion that the Doctor was probably responsible for most of the trouble anyway, and had probably kidnapped himself just to make things difficult.

'The quicker we find him the better, Brigadier. If he has any information about that alien vessel, we need it at once. Contact me as soon as you've found him.'

'How did the Security Council meeting go, General?' asked Cornish.

'Complete waste of time. They're still debating.'

'What do you think they should do?'

'Arm every available missile with atomic warheads and blast that thing out of our sky.'

Cornish looked thoughtfully at him. 'Isn't that a bit extreme, General?'

'It's our moral duty,' said Carrington fiercely, and marched stiffly out of the room.

Awkwardly the Brigadier cleared his throat. 'I think the General is a little overwrought.'

Cornish said quietly, 'I think he's insane.'

Reegan studied the tall figure stretched out on the lab table in front of him and spoke into the phone. 'No trouble at all. Your Doctor friend's as dead as a doornail.'

As he put the phone down, Liz, who was also leaning over the Doctor, loosened his collar and checking his pulse said indignantly, 'Why did you say he was dead?'

'Because it suits me.'

The Doctor opened his eyes and looked around him.

'How are you, Doctor?' asked Reegan.

'None the better for your attentions.' Slowly the Doctor sat up. 'Hello, Liz.'

'Doctor, are you all right?'

'Getting better by the minute. How about you? Have they hurt you?'

'Not really. I don't much care for the company though.'

'I don't blame you.' A little stiffly the Doctor got to his feet – and found himself staring at the alien astronauts through the glass window. 'Ah, so, there they are!'

'They're a completely alien species, Doctor.'

'Yes, I know Liz. I've been on board their ship and talked to their leader.'

Reegan was immediately interested. '*How* did you talk?'

'Their leader must have had some kind of translation machine.'

Reegan produced his black box. 'One like this?'

The Doctor took it and studied it. 'Oh no, this is only a very basic model. It only sends out signals.'

'Could you make me a better one, Doctor?' asked Reegan eagerly. 'So I could really talk to them?'

'I daresay – if I had the proper equipment. I was going to build one for myself as it happens, but I didn't get round to it.'

Reegan smiled broadly. 'Then now's your chance.'

'Why should I help you?'

'It would keep you both alive,' said Reegan reasonably.

The Doctor nodded, acknowledging that Reegan had made a very good point. 'I'll need a great deal of very expensive equipment,' he said.

With an expansive gesture, Reegan waved the Doctor to a chair. 'Make a list, Doctor.'

None of the niggling you always got from the Brigadier, thought the Doctor, as he picked up a note-pad and pencil and started to write. Reegan turned and climbed up the steps.

The Doctor rose and followed him, but Reegan was waiting at the top of the door. Shaking his head reprovingly, he said, 'Don't try it, Doctor.'

Reegan went out of the door, closing and locking it behind him and the Doctor went back to Liz. He glanced at the telephone. Liz shook her head.

The Doctor sighed. 'Is there any way out?'

'I got away once, but they caught me again. Since

then they've tightened everything up, and doubled the guards.'

The Doctor sat down at the lab desk again. 'Then I might as well get on with this list.'

'Are you really going to help him?'

In a lowered voice the Doctor said mysteriously, 'If we can't get away to the Brigadier, then we must bring the Brigadier to us.'

Before Liz could ask what he meant, the main door opened and someone came down the stairs. To Liz's astonishment, she recognised General Carrington.

For a moment she thought they'd been rescued. 'General Carrington, you've found us! How on Earth did you . . .' Her voice tailed off at the sight of the heavy service automatic in Carrington's hand.

'I think the General knew where we were all along,' said the Doctor quietly.

Carrington frowned. 'You're not surprised to see me?'

'Not particularly.'

'But I'm surprised to see you, Doctor. My instructions were that you should be killed.'

The Doctor was never averse to stirring up a bit of trouble amongst his enemies. 'Then someone disobeyed your instructions, didn't they?'

'I shall have to attend to the matter myself,' said Carrington regretfully. He raised his automatic and levelled it at the Doctor's head. 'I'm sorry, Doctor, it's my moral duty.'

Suddenly, just like Cornish before him, the Doctor realised that General Carrington was insane.

15

'We May Not Have Much More Time!'

It was Reegan who saved the Doctor's life. He came clattering down the steps just as Carrington was about to pull the trigger. 'What are you doing?'

'You told me you'd killed this man.'

'I was going to but – '

'You disobeyed an order,' said Carrington severely, as if Reegan had forgotten to polish his boots.

'I thought it was for the best.'

'You are not paid to think, Reegan,' said the General, in the best army tradition.

'He could be useful to us – '

'*I* make the decisions, Reegan.'

'Yes, sir. But he's the only one who can make a machine that will let us talk to those creatures.'

Reegan waved towards the radiation chamber where the three alien astronauts stood behind their glass window, silent spectators of events in the main lab.

'You've got a machine to do that.'

Reegan produced the little device. 'This? It only sends limited one-way signals.'

'Well?'

Reegan chose his words carefully. 'If I'm to carry out your orders efficiently, sir, I'll have to give those things some pretty complicated instructions.' He turned away with apparent indifference. 'Still, suit yourself. If you want to kill him – kill him!'

Carrington held the automatic to the Doctor's temple a moment longer. Then slowly, very slowly, he lowered it. He looked suspiciously at the Doctor. '*Could* you make such a machine?'

'Given the necessary equipment – yes.'

'And you're willing to help us?'

'That depends on what you're trying to do.'

'We have to alert the world to the menace of alien invasion,' said Carrington solemnly.

'And when do you expect this invasion?'

'At any moment!'

'I've met the leader of these aliens, General Carrington. He told me their intentions are peaceful and that those three in there are ambassadors.'

'Ambassadors!' sneered Carrington. 'That was just to put us off our guard.'

'You're convinced they're hostile?'

'Why else should they be spreading thoughout the galaxy?' said Carrington feverishly. 'They reached Mars before us.'

The Doctor nodded. 'And that's where you met them, when you were on the earlier Mars Probe?'

For a moment Carrington stared into space as he recalled the painful memory. 'They killed Jim – Jim Daniels, my fellow astronaut – simply by touching him.'

The Doctor said, 'But they didn't know then that their touch is fatal to man.'

Carrington didn't seem to hear him. 'Now they've walked into my trap. I knew that once I'd got them here I could force them to reveal their true natures.'

'So you arranged for them to send these three as ambassadors?' said the Doctor. 'Then you hired Reegan to kidnap them and use them as killers.'

Carrington nodded eagerly. 'I had to arouse public opinion.'

'And was the Minister, Quinlan, in on this?'

'Not completely. He just wanted the political glory of being the first to arrange contact with an intelligent alien species. He knew nothing of my plan to save the

126

world from their domination. He wouldn't have understood.'

'So you had him killed,' said the Doctor. 'When he was going to talk to me. What about Van Leyden and the human astronauts?'

'They knew nothing,' said Carrington decisively. 'I used them. It was the only way.'

'You've worked things out very thoroughly General,' the Doctor said.

Carrington gave the Doctor a piercing stare. 'It was the only way. You do understand that, don't you, Doctor?'

'Yes, General, I understand,' said the Doctor gently. 'You had to do what you did.'

'Exactly,' said Carrington with a kind of fierce pride. 'The world has to be protected. It's my moral duty. Will you help me?'

'I'll build your machine for you.'

'Splendid!' In command once more, Carrington turned to Reegan and said, 'I have decided to let this man live. He can be useful to us. See that he has everything he needs.'

'Yes, sir,' said Reegan solemnly.

'Oh, I shall be taking one of these creatures away with me. I've brought a shielded van. Instruct one of them to come out.'

Reegan nodded and turned to Liz. 'You – open the door!'

On the Space Centre radar screen, the large white dot that represented the alien spaceship still hung motionless. Now a small dot was moving closer towards it. This was the unmanned satellite sent up by the Americans.

'Why can't they get a picture?' asked the Brigadier.

Cornish shrugged. 'The radio pulses the thing sends out seem to be affecting the camera.'

A voice came over the loudspeaker. 'Observation satellite's instruments report intense radiation, bombardment by neutron particles.'

Suddenly the smaller dot disappeared from the screen.

Seconds later an excited voice reported, 'Space Agency are experiencing total cessation of signals from spy satellite. It is believed that the satellite has disintegrated . . .'

The telephone rang and the Brigadier picked it up. 'Yes, Lethbridge-Stewart speaking.' He listened for a moment, and then said, 'Yes, sir,' in astonished tones and put down the phone. 'It's General Carrington. He says he's captured an alien astronaut – and he's bringing it here! He wants me to arrange a nationwide telecast!'

An intricate electronic device was building up on the lab bench in front of the Doctor – but it wasn't building fast enough to satisfy Reegan. 'How long's it going to take?' he asked impatiently.

'I'm not building a crystal set, you know,' said the Doctor reproachfully.

Reegan nodded to the duty thug, who opened the door to the radiation chamber. Reegan produced his device and operated it. The two remaining astronauts began moving towards the door.

'How can I test the machine if you take them away?' demanded the Doctor indignantly.

'They'll be back. Just one or two little jobs for them.'

'More killing?'

'Only if we have to. Now, you'd better get on with it,

Doctor. I want that machine finished when I get back!'

As Reegan and the two astronauts disappeared up the stairs Liz whispered, 'You're not just going to do as he says, are you?'

'Let's get this finished,' said the Doctor quietly. 'We may not have much more time.'

Reegan's raid on the isotope store went completely according to plan. The aliens blasted open the gate and destroyed the security guards who tried to resist them. They burst open the door of the storage chamber and stood guard while Reegan's man loaded isotopes into the van.

A police car arrived as they were leaving but this too was easily dealt with.

Reegan and his men, who were all protected by radiation suits, got into the van with the astronauts and the stolen isotopes and the van drove swiftly away.

Behind on the roadway, two dead policemen lay beside their wrecked police car.

For once Michael Wakefield wasn't really looking forward to being in front of the cameras. He was supervising preparations when George Carrington marched into the broadcasting area. 'Are you ready?'

'Very soon, General.'

Two cameras were trained on a gauze-like semi-transparent screen. Behind it one could make out a bulky space-suited, helmeted figure lashed to a chair.

Wakefield gestured towards it. 'If there *is* an alien being inside that suit, General . . .'

'I can assure you there is.'

'Then doesn't it occur to you, sir, that the sight of it may create world panic – particularly with this unidentified flying object hovering above Earth?'

'We must warn the world,' said Carrington solemnly.

'Quite, sir,' said Wakefield, accepting the inevitable. 'You're sure your men will be able to remove the helmet?'

'Quite sure, Mister Wakefield.'

The Brigadier came hurrying up to them. 'Aliens have raided an isotope storage depot, sir. Many deaths, including security guards and policemen.'

Carrington turned to Wakefield. 'You see? They're already invading Earth. These creatures need radiation to live and they're willing to rob and kill to get it.'

'There were men helping them, sir.'

'Traitors, collaborators, Brigadier – like your friend, the Doctor!'

'That is an unjustified assumption, sir.'

'General Carrington,' Wakefield cut in swiftly, 'what exactly do you intend to say in your telecast? It'll be hooked up world-wide, you know.'

'I shall call on the nations of the world to unite in an attack on these creatures and their spaceship. They must be obliterated.'

Wakefield eyed the General uneasily. He liked being part of great events, but only as an onlooker, a commentator. Now it looked as if he was going to be used to start an interplanetary war . . .

The electronic lash-up on the bench in front of the Doctor was bigger now and seemed almost complete.

'Switch on the power, Liz,' said the Doctor. Liz obeyed and the machine hummed with life. 'Now, let's try and test this thing.'

Conscious of the suspicious gaze of the thug who was guarding them, Liz whispered, 'Do you think the signal will be strong enough?'

'I've boosted it as much as I can.' The Doctor raised his voice. 'Just go and stand over there, will you, Liz! See if there's any reaction.'

Liz went over the the window where the two alien astronauts, recently returned to captivity by Reegan, sat gazing out at them.

The Doctor's fingers tapped a control built into the machine, and a regular pattern of beeps began to emerge . . .

'Any reaction, Liz?'

'Not a thing!'

The Doctor beamed at the watching heavy. Then we'll just have to keep on trying, won't we?

The regular pattern of beeps went on . . .

Sergeant Benton was duty sergeant at UNIT HQ when the signal came through. The radio operator handed him a set of earphones. 'There you are, Sarge. Have a listen!'

Benton listened, then shook his head wonderingly. 'It's the old distress signal, SOS. They did away with that signal years ago.'

'Everybody's picking it up, Sarge. Taxis, police cars, fire engines. It's on a high-impulse blanket frequency.'

'See if you can get a triangulation,' ordered Benton. He grinned: 'Save Our Souls!'

Wakefield was having a quick rehearsal. 'After that, when I've introduced the General, I want you to pick him up over there, all right?'

Cornish interrupted him. 'Mister Wakefield?'

'Yes, Professor Cornish?'

'Do you think you should go ahead with the broadcast?'

'What do you mean?'

'Don't you realise what the General's going to say?'

'He's going to talk about the alien – and the unidentified flying object.'

'Yes – and he's going to call on the nations of the world to attack the spaceship, blow it out of the sky with atomic missiles. We know nothing about its powers of retaliation.'

'I daresay the General knows what he's doing,' said Wakefield hopefully. He saw the Brigadier approaching and waved him over. 'Professor Cornish is worried about the General's broadcast.'

'I'm a little worried myself,' confessed the Brigadier.

'Have you finished that machine yet, Doctor?'

'No, Mister Reegan, but we're just about to test it. Switch on, Liz.'

Liz obeyed and machine hummed with power again. The Doctor picked up an attached microphone on a long flex. He went to the display window and gazed in at the two alien astronauts.

'We are trying to convert our human speech into radio impulses and vice versa, so that we can speak and you can answer us,' he explained to them. 'Can you understand me?'

There was no response.

'Can you understand?' repeated the Doctor.

Still nothing.

'It doesn't work,' said Reegan. He slipped his hand inside his jacket. 'Sorry, Doctor. Maybe Carrington was right the first time . . .'

Suddenly a deep throaty voice crackled from the

speaker in the Doctor's machine: '*Why are we kept prisoners? Why do you make us kill?*'

Reegan snatched the mike from the Doctor. 'You will obey my orders. If you don't we'll let you die.'

'*We are ambassadors. We came in peace.*'

'Maybe so. But if you want to live you'll do exactly as you're told.' Reegan put down the mike. 'Congratulations, Doctor. Now I can make a few plans . . .'

The Doctor reached for the mike, but Reegan knocked his hand aside. 'Leave it alone!'

The Brigadier came hurrying back into the control room. 'What's happening?'

'The alien ship is transmitting to us,' said Cornish tensely. 'There's a picture coming through now . . .'

He adjusted controls and suddenly the giant monitor screen showed the blurred shape of the alien leader.

His voice boomed through the control room: '*Only a little time remains to you. We have the power to destroy your Earth. We shall use it unless our ambassadors are returned.*'

The screen went blank.

'Well, gentleman,' said General Carrington. 'Now we know exactly where we stand. We must attack – first!'

16

'We're Being Invaded!'

General Carrington marched across to the area where Wakefield had set up his TV cameras. 'I must make my broadcast at once,' he insisted.

'I'm afraid that's impossible,' protested Wakefield. 'The world-wide hook-up won't be ready for another hour yet.'

'You must get on to your people and speed things up. This is an emergency!'

Cornish moved over to Wakefield, giving him an 'I told you so' look. 'What are you going to do?' he asked.

'See if I can speed up the broadcast, of course,' said Wakefield and moved away.

The Brigadier, meanwhile, was talking to Carrington. 'Message from my HQ, sir. They've been picking up some strange SOS signals. I think there's a chance it may be the Doctor, so I intend to follow it up. If you'll excuse me, sir?'

The Brigadier was about to move away when Carrington snapped, 'Just one moment, Brigadier. 'Do you really think I don't know what's been going on?'

'Sir?'

'This Doctor of yours is in league with the enemy – and you're helping him! Security!'

Two of Carrington's military policemen came running in. 'Put this officer under arrest,' he ordered.

'I must protest, sir . . .' began the Brigadier.

'Hand over your revolver, Brigadier.'

The Brigadier unholstered his revolver and one of the MPs took it from his hand.

'I've suspected you for some time.' Carrington's

eyes were gleaming fanatically. He turned to the senior of the MPs.

'I want *all* UNIT personnel disarmed and confined to barracks and replaced by men I can trust. Take him away.'

Cornish had observed what was going on. He snatched up a phone. Carrington strode over to him. 'What do you think you're doing?'

'I'm going to get on to the Ministry.'

'Too late, Professor Cornish. All communications are now under my control.'

'This Space Centre is under *my* control, General.'

'Not any longer.'

Suddenly Cornish realised that the phone in his hand was dead.

Carrington had taken over.

The trouble with high command, reflected the Brigadier as he was marched towards his waiting staff car, was that it kept you away from the sharp end, the rough stuff. It had been quite some time since that last unarmed combat course . . .

A backwards elbow-jab disposed of one MP, and the fist of the same hand swinging forward knocked out the other. The Brigadier sprinted for the driving seat of the car, leapt inside and sped away, followed by revolver shots from the recovering MPs.

Seeing the Brigadier's staff car approaching the sentry at the main gate automatically raised the barrier, and the Brigadier shot past before the man realised anything was wrong . . .

It's no good, Sarge, I can't raise a thing,' said the UNIT radio officer. Space HQ have cut themselves right off.'

Sergeant Benton frowned. 'Keep on trying,' he

ordered, just as the Brigadier burst into the room.

'We've been trying to reach you sir,' cried Benton.

'Did you get a fix on those radio signals?'

'Yes, sir.' Sergeant Benton pointed to a wall map. 'Just about here, sir. Funny thing is, it's army land. Disused firing range and research centre. Quite near the Space Centre actually.'

'Carrington!' muttered the Brigadier. 'How many men have we, Sergeant – actually here at HQ?'

'Just a handful, sir. Most of the lads are on duty at Space HQ. Shall I recall them?'

'Too late, Benton, they'll be under arrest by now.'

'What, sir?'

Ignoring his sergeant's astonishment the Brigadier said, 'We'll have to make do with the men we've got here. You, keep that radio manned; Sergeant Benton, get me an automatic.'

'Sir!'

'Oh, and lay on some transport, will you?'

'Can't sir. Everything's over at Space HQ.'

'What!'

'Er, how did *you* get here, sir?'

'I borrowed a staff car.'

'Couldn't we use that, sir?'

'The tyres and the engine stopped quite a few bullets – I barely made it here. There must be some kind of vehicle here, Sergeant.'

'There's the Doctor's car, sir. We recovered it when Miss Shaw disappeared.'

'The Doctor's car, Benton? That's all?'

'Yessir.'

The Brigadier shuddered.

Nevertheless, a very short time later the Brigadier and the few armed men he'd been able to raise were crammed inside Bessie and jolting along a narrow country lane with Benton at the wheel.

'Stop here,' ordered the Brigadier. He peered through binoculars at a group of abandoned army huts in the middle distance. There was a low-lying brick structure a little way away from them, and outside there was parked a baker's van. The Brigadier pointed. 'That must be it!'

The little car sped off again. As they reached the bunker, two thuggish men came out of the bunker. At the sight of the Brigadier and the men, they immediately drew revolvers and opened fire.

The Brigadier and his men dived for cover, and returned fire themselves. There was a short and inconclusive gunfight which ended rather tamely when the thugs ran out of ammunition and had to surrender.

But the surrender itself had been a trick.

When the UNIT troops were close enough, their prisoners jumped them and the fighting became hand-to-hand as they struggled to get the UNIT troops' weapons.

One of the thugs went down beneath a pile of angry soldiers. The Brigadier himelf dealt with the other. After a short but satisfying fist-fight, the Brigadier delivered an uppercut that sent the thug rolling unconscious down a steep slope where he lay motionless in the mud at the bottom.

Drawing his revolver, the Brigadier led his men into the bunker.

In the underground laboratory, Reegan was doing his best to interest the Doctor in a set of plans. 'You see, Doctor? The main vault's here . . . our alien friends could blast it open in no time.'

The Doctor gave him an exasperated look. 'For the last time, I am not going to join you in a programme of systematic bank robbery.'

Reegan looked quite hurt. 'But I'm offering you an equal share, Doctor!'

He looked up as faint sounds of struggle came from outside. 'Get out there and see what's happening!'

The heavy who had been guarding Liz and the Doctor drew his revolver and headed up the steps. He ran to the top and found himself facing the Brigadier. The thug fired, missing by inches, and the Brigadier promptly shot him down.

He ran down the steps, saw Reegan drawing an automatic, and, more by accident than design, shot it out of his hand. Reegan winced, rubbed his wrist, stepped back and raised his hands. 'Make yourself at home, Brigadier!' he said wryly.

If the Brigadier expected to be greeted as a conquering hero, he was to be disappointed.

'What kept you?' demanded the Doctor irritably.

'I see you're all right, Doctor. Miss Shaw?'

'Just get me out of here,' said Liz.

The Brigadier turned to the Doctor. 'General Carrington's taken over the Space Centre. He's going to make a telecast, urging the world to attack the alien spaceship with missiles.'

'We've got to stop him!'

'Not so easy, Doctor. He's arrested most of my men and installed his own troops.'

'We've got to get in there somehow,' muttered the Doctor.

Reegan, about to be marched away by a UNIT soldier said helpfully, 'Who not use them?' He indicated the two alien figures in the radiation chamber.

The Doctor gave the Brigadier an astonished look. 'You know I think he's right!'

Reegan gave them his most engaging smile. 'You won't forget I thought of it now, will you?'

'Get him out of here!' snarled the Brigadier.

The Doctor was already at his translation machine. He adjusted controls and addressed the silent figures behind the glass window. 'We're going to return you to your own people. But first we need your help – to prevent a catastrophe . . .'

The odd-looking assault force drove up to the main gates of the Space Centre. In the lead were the Doctor, Liz, Sergeant Benton and the Brigadier, all crammed into Bessie.

The aliens and the remaining UNIT soldiers were in Reegan's baker's van close behind.

Reegan himself and his captured thugs had been locked in their own bunker to await collection.

The vehicles drew up and the occupants of Bessie jumped out. Quickly the Brigadier assessed the situation.

The barrier was down and the two heavy metal doors that gave admittance to the centre were closed and barred. They were guarded by a sizeable troop of Regular Army men, led by Carrington's MPs, all armed.

The Brigadier took a loud-hailer from one of his men. 'Open the gates!'

No one moved.

The Brigadier glanced at the Doctor, who spoke into the microphone of his translation machine: 'We are going to ask you to open these gates for us. Please try not to harm anyone.'

At a nod from the Brigadier the rear doors of Reegan's van were opened. The two silent space-suited figures stepped out and walked slowly, side by side, towards the Space Centre.

As they passed her, Liz thought that their silence, their slow movements and the black visors of their helmets made them look incredibly sinister . . .

They walked up to the barrier and flicked it upwards, advancing on towards the metal doors. For a moment

Carrington's men looked on amazed. Then several of them started to open fire.

The Doctor snatched the loud-hailer. 'Do not fire. These aliens are invulnerable to your bullets.'

Already the soldiers could see the truth of the Doctor's words. The two space-suited figures were advancing into a hail of bullets, quite unharmed.

The Doctor's voice boomed out again: 'They do not wish to harm you, but you will die if you touch them. For your own safety, please fall back. I repeat, fall back!' To the Doctor's immense relief, the astonished soldiers obeyed.

The two aliens strode side by side to the metal doors. Raising their hands, they placed them on each side of the lock area and the whole lock exploded. The doors swung back and the aliens led the way inside.

Carrington's troops drew back as the Doctor, Liz and the Brigadier and the handful of UNIT soldiers followed them.

General Carrington was preparing for his moment of supreme glory. Typically, he had taken charge, and was directing his own appearance. 'Now, Mister Wakefield, when I move over here, I want your camera to get in close on that creature. One of my men will forcibly remove its helmet. I want the world to see what these monsters are really like.'

Wakefield had long ago abdicated all responsibility for the broadcast. 'Whatever you say, General.'

Cornish made a last-minute appeal. 'General, won't you please see reason? Don't make this broadcast.'

Carrington waved him away. 'Don't interfere with matters you don't understand, Mister Cornish.'

'But you could be bringing down total destruction on us all – I believe these aliens have the powers they claim –'

'You have no concept of moral duty,' said Carrington dismissively.

'General, you must listen – '

'Security!' shouted Carrington.

Two MPs hustled the protesting Cornish away.

'Five seconds, General,' warned Wakefield.

Wakefield and the General moved to their pre-arranged camera positions. The General drew himself to attention.

The cue light winked on, and Wakefield switched on that sincere, concerned voice and manner that had made him famous – though this time the concern was perfectly genuine. Wakefield was, frankly, terrified. However, like the old pro he was, he managed not to show it as he began his opening announcement.

'Good evening. I am speaking to you from the heart of Space Control Headquarters. This telecast is being received all over the world by satellite relay . . .

Distant sounds were coming from somewhere outside the Centre – shouts and screams and the sound of gunfire. Someone was bellowing through a loudspeaker.

Like the true professional he was, Wakefield carried on: 'The world has been full of rumours about the unidentified flying object which is now hovering above our planet.'

The noise was louder now. Wakefield hestitated, caught a fierce glare from Carrington, and hurried on. 'General Carrington, Head of Space Security, himself an ex-astronaut, and veteran of an earlier Mars Probe, is about to make an announcement of tremendous importance . . .

There was a piercing scream and two terrified female technicians ran across the control room, passing right in front of camera. Wakefield winced. He signalled and the engineer cut transmission.

General Carrington was quite clear about what was

happening. Drawing his revolver he shouted, 'They're here! We're being invaded!'

As if to prove the truth of his words, two space-suited figures came stalking across the control room towards him. With a scream of terror, Carrington emptied his automatic at them, without effect.

'Security Patrols!' shrieked Carrington.

Uniformed figures flooded into the room. But they were not Carrington's MPs but UNIT troops, the Doctor and Liz in their midst. The two astronauts came to a halt and stood waiting impassively.

The Brigadier marched up to the terrified Carrington, revolver in hand. 'It's over, General Carrington. This place is now in my hands. I've released my men.'

Carrington stared wildly at him. 'But I've got to make this broadcast. It's a matter of world survival!'

'I'm sorry, General. It's my duty to place you under arrest.'

Carrington stared at him in incomprehension. 'Under arrest?'

Carrington looked round. The control room was full of silent people, and they were all staring at him.

'If you'll go with my sergeant, sir?' said the Brigadier quietly. 'Benton!'

As the Brigadier took the empty automatic from Carrington's hand, Benton stepped forward and saluted smartly. The military courtesy seemed to reassure the General. He took, hat, gloves and swagger stick from the top of a nearby console. He slipped on the gloves, put on the hat and adjusted it carefully, tucked the cane under his arm, then drew himself up to attention.

'The Sergeant will look after you, sir,' said the Brigadier.

Carrington nodded and moved away. Benton followed close behind him. He paused as he came up to the

Doctor and Liz, staring earnestly into the Doctor's face.

Somehow it seemed very important to Carrington that the Doctor at least should understand him. 'I had to do what I did, Doctor. It was my moral duty. You do understand?'

'Yes, General,' said the Doctor gently. 'I understand.'

Satisfied, Carrington marched away.

The Doctor noticed the third astronaut who was still strapped in his chair, awaiting the never-to-be made broadcast, a broadcast which might well have been the last in the history of Earth, since the insult to the alien ambassador would not have been forgiven.

Released, the third alien ambassador came to stand beside his two fellows.

Cornish, freed from custody by UNIT troops, came hurrying up to the Doctor. 'Just the man I was looking for,' said the Doctor happily. 'Now, first of all, we must send a message to the alien vessel assuring them their ambassadors are safe and well.'

There was only one thing on Cornish's mind. 'Doctor, where are my three astronauts?'

The Doctor gave him a look of mild surprise. 'My dear chap, I keep telling you, they're still up there. They're quite well and comfortable – if a bit confused! What we must do now is make an exchange, you see. We'll send their three ambassadors back up in Recovery Seven, and they'll send down our three astronauts!'

'What about the fuel problem?'

The Doctor patted him on the shoulder. 'Simple, use pure M3 variant. They won't be worried about g-force.'

Looking a little bemused, Cornish sat down in his command chair. 'This is Control,' he said. 'Get me the fuel bay.'

'Well, goodbye Mister Cornish,' said the Doctor cheerfully. 'I've got a lot of work to do in my own laboratory.'

Cornish shook hands. 'But Doctor, I'll need your help to communicate with these – ambassadors.'

The Doctor waved towards Liz. 'Well, here's Miss Shaw, she's much more practical than I am.'

Liz gave him an indignant glare. The Doctor beamed at her, gave a general nod of farewell and turned to go.

Already his mind was buzzing with speculation. That odd little incident when Liz had been caught in the time field. What if the trouble was with the dematerialisation circuit and not the time vector generator . . .

On his way out, the Doctor came up to the three silently waiting alien ambassadors, and paused for a moment. The Brigadier was standing beside them, not quite sure what to do with them, but determined not to let them out of his sight.

The Doctor nodded. 'Goodbye, Brigadier.'

'Goodbye, Doctor – and thank you.'

The Doctor hesitated a moment longer. After all, it was, in its way, an historic moment, the first formal contact between humans and an intelligent alien species. Not that the contact was likely to be the beginning of a beautiful friendship, thought the Doctor. After the fright they'd given each other the two species would probably keep well apart. The galaxy was big enough for both of them, after all.

Still, here were the three alien ambassadors, and the Doctor couldn't help thinking some little gesture was called for, some diplomatic phrase.

He held out his hand to say goodbye, then withdrew it hurriedly. 'Well, goodbye gentlemen,' he said a little awkwardly. 'Er, have a nice trip!'

Giving the three alien ambassadors a friendly nod, the Doctor went on his way.